# MARRIED TO A

# DEKALB COUNTY

# BULLY

## A Novel by

## Shanice B.

1

To submit a manuscript for our review,

email us at

submissions@majorkeypublishing.com

# <u>DEDICATION</u>

To my amazing publisher, Quiana Nicole, Thanks for all you do.

# MUSIC PLAYLIST

- **MOTORCYCLE PATCHES-** TRAVIS SCOTT AND QUAVO
- **BEST MAN-** TRAVIS SCOTT AND QUAVO
- **SAINT LAURENT MASK-** TRAVIS SCOTT AND QUAVO
- **WHERE U FROM-** TRAVIS SCOTT AND QUAVO
- **MOON ROCK-** TRAVIS SCOTT AND QUAVO
- **DANGER-** MIGOS
- **PRAY FOR LOVE-** TRAVIS SCOTT AND THE WEEKEND
- **SAINT-** TRAVIS SCOTT AND QUAVO
- **MODERN SLAVERY-** TRAVIS SCOTT AND QUAVO
- **BLACK AND CHINESE-** TRAVIS SCOTT AND QUAVO

- **BOSSES DON'T SPEAK-** MIGOS
- **BUTTERFLY EFFECT-**TRAVIS SCOTT
- **GOOSEBUMPS-** TRAVIS SCOTT
- **T-SHIRT-** MIGOS
- **KELLY PRICE-** MIGOS AND TRAVIS SCOTT
- **SLIPPERY-** MIGOS AND GUCCI MANE
- **GET RIGHT WITCHA-** MIGOS
- **DEADZ-** MIGOS AND 2CHAINZ
- **PICK UP THE PHONE-** TRAVIS SCOTT
- **DINOSAURUS-** TRAVIS SCOTT

# BOOKS BY SHANICE B.

- LOVE ME IF YOU CAN (1-3)
- WHO'S BETWEEN THE SHEETS (1-4)
- A LOVE SO DEEP: NOBODY ELSE ABOVE YOU (STANDALONE)
- LOVING MY MR. WRONG: A STREET LOVE AFFAIR (1-2)
- STACKING IT DEEP: MARRIED TO THE PAPER (STANDALONE)
- KISS ME WHERE IT HURTS (1-3)
- HE LOVES THE SAVAGE IN ME (1-2)
- LOVE, I THOUGHT YOU HAD MY BACK (STANDALONE)

# PROLOGUE
## ACE
## AUGUST 2001

I was sound asleep in my bed when my door swung open, and my mom yelled out my name. I groaned as I tried pulling the pillow back over my head. My mom hurried over to where I was sleeping and yanked the covers from my body before telling me to get my ass up. We had to go.

I didn't even have time to rub the sleep from my eyes before she was dragging me from my bed. I grumbled to myself as I grabbed my shoes on the way out. I stepped into the long hallway, and that's when I noticed my dad holding a black duffle bag in his left hand with his favorite pistol in his right.

My dad who went by the name of "Rabbit" had been in the game since he was a teenager. I had heard plenty of stories on the streets that my dad didn't show any mercy for nobody. If you were brave enough to cross him, then a bullet in your head was going to follow. One thing about Rabbit was that even though he was about that life, he didn't want me to follow in his footsteps. He always preached to me that he wanted better for me. He didn't want me to be slinging dope on the streets. Instead, he wanted me to go to college and do something with my life. He always told me that the street life didn't lead to anything but death or prison, and I believed him.

I had much respect for Rabbit, so when he told me we had to go, I didn't question the reason. I followed both of my parents to Rabbit's foreign car and was just about to hop inside when a car pulled up out of nowhere and started blasting. My mom screamed out in the distance. Everything happened so fast that I had no clue what to do. I froze, and Rabbit pulled me and my mom back into the house before slamming the door behind us. Tears fell from my eyes as shots were being fired into the house. Glass shattered as the bullets shot through the windows.

My heart was racing, and I couldn't move as Rabbit held my head down. When the shots stopped, I thought that whoever that wanted us dead was gone, but I was so wrong.

"Son, you must listen to me. Some men are about to come for me. I want you to take care of your mom and keep her safe. What I need for you to do is take this duffle bag and get the hell out of here. Run as fast as you can, and don't look back."

Never had I ever seen Rabbit cry, so when tears fell from his eyes, I knew instantly just how serious things was. I looked over at my mom who looked like she was in a trance. I slid over to her and wrapped my skinny arms around her. When Rabbit kissed her, it seemed to pull her back into reality. She begged for him to come along with us, but he shook his head and said he couldn't.

"Take care of our son, Myra, and remember that I love you."

My heart broke when the door was kicked in a few moments later. I knew it was time to leave, or nobody was going to make it out alive. I grabbed the duffle bag and pulled mom by the arm as we ran out the back door. When we heard gunshots followed by silence, I knew in my heart that Rabbit was gone. Mom's sobbing filled my ears as we ran for our lives. The black duffle bag weighed down on my ten-year-old frame, but I didn't dare stop. There was no time for me to cry about Rabbit; I had to get us somewhere safe. It was pitch dark outside, and we barely had any light to see, but Mom and I ran over two miles before we came to an abandoned farmhouse. We headed inside and closed the door behind us. I prayed that we stayed safe until morning.

I was grateful that it was summertime, and it wasn't cold outside because we probably would have frozen to death. Mom didn't speak, and I didn't bother by saying anything directly to her. I knew she was probably hurting because I surely was. Instead of trying to console my mom, I unzipped the black duffle bag and was shocked to see it filled with nothing but stacks of money.

I was speechless. Just when I found my voice to ask my mom about the money, that's when she found her voice.

"I told Rabbit not to do it. I begged him to get out the business, but he wouldn't listen to me. Now, he's dead!" my mom cried out.

I scooted over to where she was sitting and held her as she cried on my small shoulder.

"It's going to be okay, Mom. I'm going to take care of

you. I promise you."

As my mom cried,  I realized I was all my mom had, and there was no way I was ever going to leave her side.

# CHAPTER 1

## ACE

## NOVEMBER 2006

I had just turned fifteen today, and I couldn't stop the tears from falling. If I had one wish, I would have wished that Rabbit would have been there to celebrate it with me. It was eight in the evening, and I had just come back from my Uncle Dro's house. I had spent the day with my little cousin, Rocco. We had gotten high all damn day, ate pizza, and had watched a football game.

Time I stepped into the house, I already knew my mom was up to some bullshit because the lights were cut off when I tried to flip the switch. Damn, I could have sworn I had given her the money to go pay the light bill last week, but apparently, she didn't do it. I groaned with frustration as I shivered from the coldness that was in the air.

I called out my mom's name, but I got no answer. I walked throughout the four-bedroom house, but my mom was nowhere to be found. I eventually gave up looking for her and pulled out my cell to see if she was going to answer her phone. Her phone went straight to voicemail. There was no way I was about to sit up in this cold ass house with no lights or heat. I was just about to take my ass back down the road to Rocco's spot when my mom stepped her ass through the door. I groaned with irritation when I noticed that she could barely stand up.

For the past five years, I had been doing what I could to stand by my mom and make sure she was straight, but she still wasn't happy. She was suffering from some very serious depression and had started drinking heavily. I had tried talking to her on numerous occasions on getting some help, but she always told me she didn't need it.

I shook my head at her as I noticed the bottle of liquor in her hand. I walked over to her, took the bottle from her, and placed it on the table.

"Mom, did you pay the light bill?"

She stared at me with bloodshot eyes before shaking her head.

"What did you do with the two hundred dollars I gave you for the lights?"

She didn't speak, which really irritated me because I

was doing my best to keep a roof over our heads. It was only so much I could do since I was a minor.

"Mom, I'm doing everything in my power to take care of us, but I can't do this if you don't get your shit together!" I screamed at her.

Never had I ever cursed at her, but it was a first time for everything. When she started crying, my heart broke because I had completely just disrespected her. I counted to ten before I grabbed her and embraced her in a hug.

"I can't do this, Ace. I can't live without Rabbit."

"Mom, please just stop it. I got you. I've been having your back since I was ten."

"I love you, son. I honestly do. But every day when I wake up to an empty bed, I secretly wish that I would have stayed with him."

"But… I wouldn't have a mother if you would have stayed."

This made my mother cry harder. My heart was aching because I knew the pain that she was going through. There was never a day that went by that I wasn't thinking about Rabbit. I held her as her slim body shook from her crying.

She finally pulled away a few moments later with a weak smile on her face.

"Thanks for being such an amazing son. You're all I have left."

I watched as she opened her Tequila and began to drink it straight.

"Mom, we ain't got no lights. Pack a bag so we can go stay with Uncle Dro."

Mom rolled her eyes at my statement.

"I don't understand why your ass always mentioning your uncle name in this damn house. He is dead to me. He's part of the reason why your father ain't here. He was the one who got your father so heavy in the streets. I ain't going no damn where, but you can pack your shit and go if you want to," my mom snapped.

Every time I mentioned anything about Uncle Dro, I always got that reaction. I understood her hate toward my uncle, but at the end of the day, that man was family. Uncle Dro couldn't make Rabbit do anything that he didn't want to do. That was what my mom failed to realize. Instead of fussing with her, I decided to leave the topic alone.

"Happy birthday," she mumbled to me before she headed toward her room, slamming the door behind her. I headed toward my room and packed a bag. I didn't even bother telling her that I was gone.

*******

**A Few Days Later**

When my alarm went off, I put the alarm on mute and closed my eyes tightly. I wasn't in the mood to go to school, but staying home wasn't an option. Today was Rabbit's birthday, and it was the most emotional day of the year. If I didn't have to take a test, I would have rolled back over and slept the day away, but I eventually slid out of bed so I could get dressed for school.

For the past couple of days, my mom had barely come out her room. She only came out to take a bath and eat. I took it upon myself to start doing the cooking and cleaning to help her out more around the house. For the past few days, I heard her cry herself to sleep every night. It hurt me to my soul to know my mom was so unhappy.

After I was done getting dressed for school, I tiptoed

into her room. She was lying in bed lightly snoring. I gently moved her long black hair out her face as I bent down and placed a kiss on her cheek.

"I love you, Mom," I mumbled before placing my book bag over my shoulder and heading out the door.

Rocco was standing outside waiting for me. He joked around with me to cheer me up, but I wasn't in the mood. The whole walk to school I said nothing I only listened to Rocco and only shook responded when he really wanted to know my opinion on something.

The whole day at school I was spaced the fuck out. I wanted nothing more than to wake up from this horrible nightmare to learn that all my heartache was a dream, but I was sadly disappointed to find that this was all a reality. Rabbit was gone, and he was never going to come back. If I had one wish, I would bring my dad back to life and make my mother happy again.

I was relieved when the end of the day finally came. When the bell ranged, I hurried out front, so I could meet up with Rocco. We dapped one another up before we started on our two-mile walk toward home. As we walked, we talked about our day and the girl in our history class that Rocco was crushing on. I listened to him without interrupting, even though my mind was somewhere else.

"Ace, you good, bro?"

"Yeah, I'm good, but I need to hurry home. Something ain't right," I mumbled to him.

I didn't even give Rocco time to respond before I took off down the road to my house. Mom and I lived in a two-hundred-thousand-dollar home down the road from Uncle Dro's house, which was around the same price. After Rabbit died, Mom bought a house, a black Jaguar, and promised me my first car when I turned sixteen. I only had one more year before I was driving an all-black Benz. The money that Rabbit had given me that night was enough for me and Mom to never have to worry about struggling or asking anybody for shit.

As I ran home, the cold wind hit my face with a vengeance. A few moments later, I was pushing the front door open and was yelling out my mom's name. I got no answer. I pulled off my book bag, headed toward her room, and pushed open her door. Tears fell from my eyes when I saw her laying on the floor with a bullet in her head. I stared down at the woman who I loved with all my heart and soul, and it tore me apart to know she had taken her own life.

I wanted to touch her, to hold her, but I couldn't bring myself to do it. The gun was in her hand, and her eyes were wide open as she lay in a pool of her own blood. I wiped the rest of my tears from my eyes when I heard the ambulance in the distance. I had been so engrossed at looking at her that I didn't even notice that Rocco was standing next to me. I guess he had stepped in and called 911. When the EMT's burst into the room, I moved aside as they came to remove her body.

Rocco was there with me every step of the way as they zipped my mom's limp body in a body bag. I answered a few questions that the cops insisted I answer before Uncle Dro pulled up in his black Bentley Truck and told the cops to get the fuck out my face. Here I was thinking that the cops were going to say something to Uncle Dro, but instead of making a scene, the cops decided to leave me alone. Uncle Dro had a name in the streets. He ran the city of Decatur and had cops, judges, lawyers, and even the mayor on his payroll. He wasn't the type of nigga you wanted to cross or fuck with. I was grateful when the police told me I could leave, and they didn't have any more questions to ask me.

I hopped in the back of Uncle Dro's Bentley truck while Rocco rode in the front. Everyone was quiet, and I was thankful. I had lost not only my dad, but now my mom. I was an orphan. I couldn't stop the tears from falling. I didn't give a fuck about anybody saying it was weak for a nigga to cry. I was forever going to cry for the death of my parents. I knew, deep in my heart, that my mother missed Rabbit way too damn much to live any longer, but damn, I thought she would at least stay here with me until I was fully grown.

I was angry and hurt that she had left me like she had. I felt she was selfish as hell for that shit. As I continued to stare out the window, I did what I could to get my emotions in check. It was time that I realized that this was my life, and I was going to have to accept the shit whether I wanted to or not.

# CHAPTER 2

# HARMONY

## 2017

As I stared into the mirror, I couldn't help but feel disgusted by my appearance. I was rocking two black eyes with a busted lip, a nasty bruise on my cheek and my collarbone. I no longer had the coke bottle figure that I used to have and cherished. I was slimming down more each month and I wasn't even on a diet plan. I was just that depressed and stressed. Tears fell from my eyes because this wasn't supposed to have been my life. I never thought that Kannon could ever hurt me like he was doing, but I had been so wrong. I met him when I was only eighteen years old, and he was twenty. I fell deeply in love with this nigga, not because of all the money that he was stacking, but because I felt like I was getting a good thing. I was young, crazy, and was fresh out of high school. I was looking for love to escape the abuse that I was dealing with at home. Never did I ever think that I was running into a monster who was going to make my life a living hell.

When Kannon and I first met, he treated me like a damn queen. I didn't have to lift a finger or ask him for shit. That nigga took good care of me. Bitches were hating hard as hell on me because they couldn't understand why he had decided to fuck with me when he could have had any bad bitch that he wanted. When I told that nigga I wanted to go to college to become a teacher, he didn't hesitate to pay my tuition so I could attend Perimeter College and get my Associate's Degree in Education. That nigga held me down, moved me out my mama's abusive household, and encouraged me every step of the way to follow my dreams.

The first time that nigga laid his hands on me, I blamed it on the fact that he was wasted and didn't know what he was doing, but the abuse didn't stop there. It continued and even got worse. A slap turned into a punch; a punch turned into broken ribs, a broken jaw, and bruises that I had to cover with heavy make-up. So here I was, standing in my bathroom, crying my eyes out because I didn't know what to do with my life. Growing up, my life was already hard enough, and here I was suffering the same abuse that I received at home, but the only difference was it wasn't from my mama but from the nigga I thought loved me.

I wish I had listened to my girl Bria when she told me to leave his ass when he first laid hands on me. The fact that Bria never liked Kannon and didn't have shit good to say about him was the only reason I didn't listen to her ass when it came to my relationship. Even though she meant well, I tried never to dwell on anything that she told me. My hands shook as I tried picking up my phone from off the bathroom sink so I could call her and tell her what had just gone down. Her phone rung close to three times before I finally heard her voice.

When I heard Tay in the background moaning and telling her to ride his dick faster, I was about to hang up because apparently, I had called at the wrong time.

"Bitch, what you want?" Bria asked as she breathed loudly into the phone.

"It's about Kannon."

Bria must have stopped what she was doing because I could hear Tay grumbling in the background about not being able to catch his nut.

"Bria, I will just call you back."

"Fuck no. Tay will be fine. I have been giving him pussy all damn day. He can wait until I talk to you."

If I wouldn't have been hurting, I would have laughed at her craziness, but how I was feeling at the moment laughing was the last thing I wanted to do.

"Now, tell me what that nigga Kannon did."

"I just found out he fucking the bitch up the road from us. We got to fighting." I cried into the phone.

"Harmony, you just need to pack your shit up and get ghost on his ass. You too damn beautiful to be letting that nigga take you through all that shit he taking you through. You got too much shit going for yourself."

"But, I can't leave. I owe him."

"Hold the fuck up. What the hell do you owe his ass? Listen to yourself. You letting that nigga brainwash your ass. Leave all that shit that he got you, and come stay with me. You know you like a sister to me. Don't keep on letting that nigga fuck you over."

Tears fell down my cheeks because I knew Bria was spitting some real shit. I just wasn't prepared to up and dip

29

out on Kannon. I was hoping that one day he was going to change back to the nigga who I first met six years prior.

"He can take everything from you, but he can't take that education back that he paid for you to have. If I was you, I would dip. I bet you over there rocking you a black eye and a busted lip."

I grew quiet, and Bria took my silence that she was correct.

"Where that nigga at? I will let Tay and his goons take care of his pussy ass."

"No, you won't. Bria, I can handle myself."

"I love you, Harmony, but I'm not going to get involved if you don't want me to. If you want him dead, just let me know. I will let Tay handle his ass, and if he won't do it I won't mind putting a bullet in his head for you."

I quickly tried to rush Bria off the phone when I heard Kannon's voice calling out my name.

"Bria, I got to go. Kannon just got home."

I hurried to cut off the bathroom light and headed downstairs to see what he wanted. I was relieved when I noticed that he was in a better mood than before he left. I still couldn't get over the insults he threw at me when I found out about him fucking the bitch up the road from our house. He placed a kiss on my bruised cheek before pulling me into an embrace.

My skin began to crawl as he began to caress my bruised body. I didn't know what to expect from him most days. His temper was erratic as hell. I was beginning to think the nigga was bipolar or had a personality disorder. I let him hold me until he pulled away and headed upstairs. He claimed he was tired and had to get up in a few hours to take care of some business. He turned back toward me and told me to come upstairs with him. I nodded my head and followed behind him. As we laid together in bed, I began to wonder what would happen if I ever tried to leave him. Would he let me go, or would he put up a fight? I quickly wiped my tears away from my bruised cheek. I was tired of the beatings, and the fact he had started cheating was something I couldn't tolerate. I silently turned away from his snoring body and cried myself to sleep.

\*\*\*\*\*\*\*

I woke up a few hours later to an empty bed. I stared at my clock and noticed that it was seven in the morning. I groaned as I slid out of bed and headed toward the bathroom so I could start getting dressed for work. A few months ago, I landed a job at a daycare called Sandy's Daycare. I couldn't lie—I hated my job with a damn passion. The pay was awful, and the fact we were short staffed didn't make the shit any better. I had wanted to walk off my job plenty of times, but I always talked myself out of it because Kannon had paid some good ass money for my tuition to get my degree, so there was no way I was about to let my education go to waste. Even though he told me that he didn't care if I came back home, I wasn't stupid enough to listen to him. What I found depressing was that if he decided to put my ass out, I didn't even make enough money to take care of myself. I had struggled all my damn life I was tired of struggling. I loved the fact that Kannon was giving me all the material things that I used to lay in bed and dream about. I was driving a damn Beamer and was living in a four-hundred-thousand-dollar home with four bedrooms, three bathrooms, and a patio with an in-ground pool outside. Kannon made sure that I didn't want for anything, and that's what I loved about him.

He knew how to take care of business. He also was sexy as hell. He had bitches at my job just staring at his ass whenever he came to drop me off lunch if I couldn't go to get it myself. He was tall, rocked a low fade, he was clean shaved, slim, dark-skinned with pretty white teeth, and resembled the actor Lance Gross who played on Tyler Perry's *House of Payne.*

After stepping out the shower, I hurried to put on my clothes because I didn't want to get caught up in traffic. I wasn't in the mood to hear my supervisor, Mrs. Taylor, bitching and complaining about me being late. I applied a heavy amount of makeup to my caramel complexion and put on a little eyeliner and mascara just before I flat ironed my Remy hair weave. After I was fully dressed, I stared at my reflection in the mirror to make sure I was on point. I double checked my makeup and was glad when I noticed that all my bruises had been covered. There was no way in hell that I wanted any of them bitches at work to get a glimpse of what my face really looked like. That shit wasn't going to lead to nothing but gossip and some little bitch getting her feelings hurt if they stepped to me with the bullshit and the fake concerns. I had always been a private person and one thing I couldn't stand were a nosy ass bitch.

I grabbed my iPhone, hopped in my candy apple red Beamer, and cruised to work.

I wasn't even at work a good hour before one of my coworkers named Jordan started in on my ass. I swear that bitch had it out for me. She constantly was checking for me and was always lying about some shit. I swear I hated a liar, and that bitch lied as easily as she breathed. She lied on everyone, there was no bitch there that haven't been lied on. I had no clue how the fuck she kept her job. Even though I hated my job with a passion, I made sure to bring my ass to work every day. Never had Mrs. Taylor ever been the type to come into our rooms to see what we were doing with the kids. She always stayed in her office and watched us on the cameras while she did her paperwork, but when Mrs. Taylor started coming in and out my room to watch everything that I was doing, I knew instantly that Jordan's hoe ass had something to do with it. She was always trying to cut somebody's throat, and she cut mines with no hesitation. Jordan was the only bitch who was making all the money and the hoe still wasn't happy.

She still was finding shit to irritate me with. I hated to see the bitch coming.

I rolled my eyes as she came into my classroom, trying to tell me what to damn do about the kids that I was keeping. I quickly dismissed her ass and told her politely that she wasn't my boss, and I wasn't about to listen to her ass. She quickly took the hint and got the fuck on. I swear if I didn't need my damn job, I would have been dragged her ass up and down the hallway of that daycare center. But I needed my job, and I wasn't about to serve no jail time for that crazy hoe.

Every time she stepped foot in my class, all the kids always started to cry on her ass. When we would have to work each other's rooms sometimes due to being short staffed, those babies would give her ass the business. I guess because she was evil as hell. The kids knew she wasn't about shit. In my room, I was keeping infants as well as one-year-olds. I loved them, and I got along with the parents as well. A few of the parents had taken a few of the kids out of the daycare due to not being able to get along with Mrs. Taylor and Jordan's crazy ass. Both of them were full of shit, but that was just my opinion.

The whole day went by slow as hell, and I was literally crawling up the wall from all the favoritism that Mrs. Taylor was showing to Jordan's fake ass. I had just finished feeding the babies and was about to lay them down for a nap when Mrs. Taylor walked her ass into my room.

"Harmony, you can go and take your lunch break. Jordan is going to cover your class until you come back. You have one hour for lunch."

I eyed the Indian bitch up like she was crazy. There was no way I was about to leave my babies with Jordan's crazy ass. The babies didn't even like her ass, and they weren't going to do anything but scream the whole time that I was going to be gone.

Even though I didn't want to leave, I decided to go

without a fuss. I grabbed my purse, and I wasn't even out the door all the way before the babies started crying all at once. I said a silent prayer as I pulled my Gucci shades over my eyes and headed out the door. I was just about to hop in my Beamer when Kannon pulled up next to me in his black Rolls Royce.

"Hey, baby, hop in. We can have lunch together."

I hopped in his truck and leaned back in the seat as his hands began to caress my thighs. I sort of froze and squeezed my eyes shut. These days I had no clue which Kannon I was going to see. He had so many sides of him that he always kept me guessing. As he caressed my thighs with his hand I tried to relax and let the romantic side of Kannon take control.

We pulled up at the Chinese restaurant called Wonder Wok ten minutes later, and I gladly hopped out. I was hungry as hell and was glad to finally be away from work, even if it was only for an hour. As we ate our food, Kannon and I laughed and talked with one another like old times. Damn, I missed him when he acted like this. I was grateful he wasn't in a foul mood and he wasn't trying to start an argument over some dumb shit. I was thankful that today he was acting like he had some sense. The fact that I was dealing with that crazy ass low paying job then coming home to Kannon was beginning to stress a bitch out.

"Baby, I need to talk to you about some important shit."

I stopped eating, placed my fork down on my plate, and stared into his soft brown eyes.

"Harmony, I know I have done some foul shit to you—beating you, talking down to you at times, and cheating on you. It was wrong of me to treat you like that. You didn't deserve that shit. I just want to take this time to tell you that I'm sorry for all the abuse that I have inflicted on you. I truly love you, and I don't see myself with anyone but you. My life would be worthless and wouldn't mean shit if I didn't have you in my life to show me this unconditional love that you have shown me from day one. I know I'm not perfect, and I have issues that I have to deal with, but I'm willing to work on myself. I'm willing to do what I have to do to keep you in my life, baby."

Tears were welling up in his eyes, and I was

speechless. Never had Kannon ever said some shit like this again. I couldn't even wrap my mind around any of it.

"I just want to make things like how it used to be."

"I miss how things used to be also," I replied softly.

He touched my chin before placing a small kiss on my lips. When he broke the kiss, he quickly dug into his pocket and pulled out a black velvet box. My heart began to race as he stood up in front of me and bent down on one knee.

"I love you, Harmony. You mean the world to me. I want to spend the rest of my life with you. Will you marry me?"

Tears fell down my cheeks as I covered my mouth with my right hand. The restaurant was packed as hell, so all eyes were on us, and people were waiting to see just what I was about to say. Even though I couldn't speak, I nodded my head to let him know that I was all for marrying him. My left hand shook as he slid the diamond ring on my finger. I didn't know how much he had spent on the ring, but it was so beautiful.

After he had slid the ring on my finger, our lips caressed one another, and his tongue slid down my throat.

Everyone in the restaurant clapped and shouted out "congratulations!"

My whole body felt as if I was at an all-time high. When I looked back at Kannon, I felt in my heart that he was ready to do better and treat me like the queen that I was. All the hurt that Kannon had caused me was now a distant memory. I prayed that I was making the right decision and wouldn't later regret it.

# CHAPTER 3

## ACE

I had just left the trap house when my phone began to blast Travis Scott. I looked down at the phone and picked it up when I saw my cousin Rocco's name pop up on the screen.

"Bro, where the hell you at?"

I could hear the stress in his voice, so my mind instantly went on alert that something was going on.

"I'm leaving the trap house. What's wrong?"

"Nigga, you need to get your ass down here at the North Dekalb Medical Center. I'm up here with Dad. Something going on with him, man."

"Give me twenty minutes, and I will be pulling up. Y'all in a room yet?"

"Yeah. We in room 233."

"Okay. Don't stress, bro. I'm on the way," I reassured him.

I didn't hesitate to whip my midnight blue Aston Martin around and head north so I could see what was up with my uncle Dro. After Rabbit died, my uncle was the closest thing I had left to a father figure for me. After my mom killed herself, my uncle stepped in and raised me like I was his own. Rocco and I had always been close growing up, but we got even closer when I moved in with him when I was only fifteen. I looked at him more like a brother than a cousin. My mind was running a mile a minute because Rocco and Uncle Dro were all the family I had left. There was no way I was ready to lose either one of them.

For the past two years, Uncle Dro had been going back and forth to the hospital, battling lung cancer. His health was deteriorating, which only put a strain on Rocco. Rocco and I had started to hit the streets harder than ever, even though Uncle Dro begged us to leave the street life alone. I understood he wanted us to get an education and leave the street shit for someone else, but it was in our blood to be in the streets, and it was nothing that I could do to change that shit.

When I first went to live with my uncle, he was still running the streets and getting that fast money. When I turned sixteen, Rocco and I started selling dope on the block. It only lasted a month before he found out and lit our ass on fire. He sat us down and told us both that he wanted more for us, but it went in one ear and out the other. When we turned seventeen, Rocco and I got kicked out of high school for selling weed to some of the students in the school. Uncle Dro's money did the talking for us to get back in school, but Rocco and I weren't bothered by that shit right then. We eventually stopped going to high school and went to get our GED instead.

I pulled up at the hospital in less than twenty minutes and headed inside. I got on the elevator and pressed the button for the second floor. When I stepped into the room, Rocco was sitting beside a sleeping Uncle Dro.

"Bro, what's going on?"

Rocco looked up at me, and I could see the tears in his eyes. Rocco was never the type of nigga to cry, so I knew whatever he was about to say to me was serious.

"He's dying, bro. He's in his last stage of lung cancer."

I walked over to Rocco and embraced him in a brotherly hug. My heart felt heavy as hell.

"No, this can't be true," I mumbled to myself as I took a seat in the chair that was next to Rocco's. I looked at my uncle, and that's when I noticed that he looked frail. My uncle always had been a slim ass nigga, so I never thought anything of it. My uncle looked like a pale ass banana with dark circles under his eyes like he hadn't slept in days. Tears fell from my eyes, and I wiped them away. Damn, I swear everyone that I cared about always ended up being taken away from me. I looked at Rocco, and he stared back at me. He must have been thinking the same thing because he quickly told me that we were all each other had.

I had been sitting in the same spot for over an hour before my uncle finally woke up. He coughed, and I handed him a small cup of water. I watched him as he took a few sips and then put it back on his tray.

The nurse walked in a few moments later and asked if he was ready for lunch. He quickly nodded his head and told her that he was indeed ready to eat. After the nurse disappeared, Uncle Dro looked over at Rocco and then at me.

"I want y'all to both know that I love y'all," Uncle Dro said with a raspy voice.

He looked at me for a few moments before saying,

"Ace, even though you ain't my biological son, I feel like you are. My brother would be proud to see how you've grown up to a fine gentleman."

Tears began to well in my eyes.

"Ace before I die, I think it's time for you to know what truly happened to your father."

"No, Dad, don't talk like that. You ain't about to die," Rocco cut in.

"Rocco, I've accepted my fate. I'm fifty-three years old. I've lived my life. I'm tired of fighting this cancer. I'm going to be okay. I just want y'all to live life to the fullest because you never know when it's going to be your last."

When Uncle Dro's eyes cut back toward me, my heart began to beat erratically. I felt as if it was about to fall out my damn chest. For years, I had wanted to know what happened, and I was finally about to learn the truth.

"When your father was killed, I blamed myself, and I guess your mother blamed me also because after your father died, she didn't want to have shit to do with me. Your father and I had always lived the street life since we were ten years old. We had to do what we had to do. We didn't grow up with the shit that you and Rocco grew up with. We never had time to enjoy being kids because we were doing what grown niggas were doing and that was hustling. Our parents were part of the reason your father and I chose the street life. They were nothing but two crackheads looking for their next fix. The streets raised us, not our parents."

Uncle Dro licked his lips and became quiet for only a moment before he began to tell me more.

"When your father met your mother, it was love at first sight. Back then, I didn't believe in that bullshit, so I clowned his ass for falling in love with a girl like your mother. Your mother wasn't on his level, and I'm not saying that in a bad way. But she wasn't about that street life. She was smart as hell and had a college education. Her parents hated your father because of his lifestyle so they never accepted him as part of their family. When your mother got married and had you, her parents disowned her, and she clung to your father, and they became as one."

A smile crossed my uncle's face.

"She really made my brother happy, and for that, I had

nothing but respect for your mother. After he got married, I noticed a change in him. He began to change for the better, and I hated it. He wanted to go legit, but I wasn't ready at the time. I had so much shit that I wanted to do before I even thought that way. We had a few disagreements, and we stopped talking for a few months over the shit, but eventually, he came back around. By that time, a few niggas had just moved from New Orleans and were trying to take over. There was no way I was about to let no outside niggas come to Decatur and fuck up my paper. When my money started being affected, I knew what I had to do to get rid of them."

Uncle Dro coughed a few times before he sipped on his small cup of water and began talking again.

"Your father begged me to leave the New Orleans niggas alone and get off the corner, but I didn't want to hear that shit. I wanted them off my turf, and I was willing to spill blood if I had to. I came up with the scheme of robbing those niggas of all their merchandise, and I talked your father into going along with me. After he found out how much money was going to be involved, he quickly agreed. At the time, he said he was doing it to secure your future. Everything that Rabbit did when he was alive was for you and your mom," he said sadly.

Your father and I hit them niggas where it hurt and killed all of them, so there was no evidence or witnesses to tell shit, but one of the niggas just happened to survive. He dipped out of Decatur, but I didn't give a damn because I was back making my money. A month later, word on the streets was that the New Orleans niggas were on their way to fuck some shit up, but at first, I didn't believe the hype, so I kept on doing what I had to do. Your father took the money that we found, and I took the drugs and the guns and sold all that shit on the streets."

Rocco and I didn't say shit as my uncle got deeper into the story.

"A week before your father was killed, I flew out of town to meet up with some niggas from Chi-Town that were interested in doing business with me. When I got back, I learned that them New Orleans niggas had come through, and they were the ones responsible for your father's death."

I didn't speak. I just sat back in my seat as I absorbed all that information. My heart felt heavy, and I didn't know if I needed to be angry at my uncle or not.

"I know you may hate me," he mumbled as he began to cry.

"I don't hate you. I just hate my dad had to be the one to die."

"Every day, I think that if I would never have dragged your father back into the streets, he and your mom would probably still be alive today. Your mama died hating me."

I didn't correct him because it was true. She hated Uncle Dro with a passion.

Uncle Dro was just about to say more, but that's when the nurse came in and brought his tray. After he had finished eating, he ended up dozing back off to sleep. I sat there for most of the day with Rocco and him before my phone began to vibrate in my pocket. I groaned when I noticed it was Crystal calling. I quickly sent that bitch to voicemail. I wasn't in the mood to hear her bitching.

Crystal and I had only been talking for about three months, and she was already asking me if I was ready to make it official. That wasn't happening any time soon with anyone. I wasn't ready to get into a serious relationship with nobody.

I was far from crazy. I knew why Crystal wanted to fuck with me, and that was because I was making major moves in the streets. I could give her all the lavish shit her heart desired. When a nigga had money and was making major moves, bitches swarmed to you like flies. I wasn't no ugly nigga either. I was dark chocolate in complexion and stood about six feet three. I rocked a low fade and a trimmed beard that had bitches dropping their panties without giving a second thought. Because of my looks, bitches always felt like they were in love with my ass when they really were more in love with what I could do for them.

Not once had I met a bitch who wasn't trying to make a come up through me. All I did was give these hoes some good dick and sent them on their way. I wasn't about to give no bitch my heart when she showed signs that she was a gold digger. That would be stupid on my part. I kept my heart close to my chest, and I was going to keep it that way until I met the woman who was for me.

I was just about to get ready to leave the room so I could head to the house when Rocco's phone began to ring. I noticed the irritated look on his face just before he picked up the phone to say hello. I knew even before he picked it up that it was probably his baby's mama, London, calling him on some bullshit. When Rocco started cursing into the phone, I just stared at his ass. I was thankful that I didn't have any kids with any crazy ass hoes. He stayed on the phone for over ten minutes going back and forth with her ass. When he hung up on her ass, I eyed his ass up.

"Nigga, you good?"

"Hell nah, I ain't good. If I could, I would kill that bitch with her crazy ass."

"Man, you need to calm down," I told him.

"Nigga, you can't tell me to calm down. You ain't got no baby by that crazy bitch."

I laughed at his ass because he was big mad over some bullshit.

"What she talking about now?"

"She talking about she ain't going to let me see Jasmine

on her birthday next week."

"Nigga, what you do for her to say she won't let you see her?"

Rocco looked at me and was just about to lie, but I guess he thought twice about it.

"I sort of went over there and broke her off some dick, and now, she acting crazy as hell."

I looked back at Rocco and shook my head.

"Nigga, you doing some dangerous ass shit. Out of all the women to fuck with, why are you gonna fuck around with your ghetto ass baby mama? You know she will ruin you if she got the chance. You just gave her the ammunition to use on your ass."

"I know, Ace. Damn, you don't think I know I fucked up? But I ain't going to lie. Even though my baby mama ratchet as hell, her pussy is A1."

"Okay. Well, I hope it was worth it, nigga. Because if you ain't careful, she will make your life a living hell."

"Man, I don't know what to do."

"I don't know what to tell your ass either, because you always fucking around with hoes who ain't got shit to lose."

"You need to start fucking with females who know their place, and London isn't in that category."

Rocco was light skinned just like Uncle Dro. He was about five feet ten and rocked dreads that stopped past his shoulders. A few months ago, he got a gold grill in his mouth and tried to talk me to into getting it in my mouth also. I quickly told his ass I was good. I didn't want all that gold and silver in my damn mouth. I guess when females saw Rocco, they instantly saw money, and they flocked to his ass. Ever since I had known Rocco, he had never been faithful to no bitch. He always had more than one bitch who he was dicking down. He was too deeply involved in the streets to even give a fuck about a bitch besides his trifling ass baby mama.

Rocco and I talked about his situation for a while longer before he finally asked me if I would pick up Jasmine from daycare on her birthday.

"Nigga, didn't London tell your ass you can't see her."

"Fuck London. I'm going to pick my baby up from daycare like I do every day. I wish she might say some fuck shit about it. Are you going to go pick her up for me or not?" Rocco asked quizzically.

"Why you can't pick her up again?" I joked.

"I gotta make a run, so I ain't going to be back in town in time to pick her up."

"Well, I got you, bro. I will pick her up for you, but London better not call my phone with that crazy shit."

"Nah, she likes you, bro. She just doesn't care for me like that," Rocco mumbled.

"Nigga, stop all that damn lying. Y'all wouldn't still be fucking if she ain't like you."

Rocco smirked before he dapped me up.

"Thank you, bro, for being here and helping me out."

"Of course, I'ma always be here," I replied truthfully.

# CHAPTER 4

# HARMONY

"Bitch, the ring looks nice, but I don't think you need to trust this nigga," Bria declared as she and I dug into our barbecue sandwiches at Moe's BBQ.

"Bria, I know what you mean, but I really think that Kannon has changed or at least is trying to do better."

Bria snorted before popping a fry in her mouth.

"When I go to church Sunday, I'm going to make sure I pray to the Lord to give you some guidance because, baby, you going to need it if you planning on actually marrying Kannon."

"Bria, for once, can you stop the hate?"

Bria nearly choked and looked at me angrily before she placed her lemonade back on the table.

"Bitch, are you really trying to kill me up in here? Because them words you just said nearly choked my ass. What you and Kannon have together isn't anything to be jealous of. And no, I'm not trying to down you, sis, or talk bad about your ass because my relationship isn't A1 either, but when a nigga causing pain to my sister by beating her to the point where she rocking bruises, then that's a problem in my book. You don't deserve that shit."

"Bria…"

She held her hand up, so I closed my mouth to let her talk.

"I've told you since day one that Kannon ain't about no business, and yet and still, you deal with him and let him hit you. I just don't want to wake up one day, and he has killed you. Just think carefully about what you doing, boo. You only get one life to live."

Instead of fussing with Bria about my relationship, I decided to take the time to enjoy my lunch before I had to head back to that awful place that I called a job.

Since I'd known Bria, she had always been the one who didn't take shit from no one. I mean, she was quick to fuck a nigga up if he even thought about crossing her. I had nothing but respect for her, but all I wanted her to do was stop harassing me about my relationship with Kannon.

We almost finished eating our meals when a nigga came up to our table and started to try to spit game at Bria. I watched as Bria flirted back but quickly shot the nigga down when he asked for her number. I waited until the nigga had walked off before I burst out laughing at her ass.

"Bitch, I don't know why you like playing with these niggas like you want them."

Bria smirked before she sipped on her lemonade.

"Ain't that what niggas do to us females? I'm only doing what they do."

I wiped the tears from my eyes from laughing at her ass for straight up dismissing the nigga. He left our table with hurt feelings.

Bria wasn't anywhere near ugly, so she always had niggas up in her face trying to holler at her ass, and she would quickly shut all their asses down. Bria was brown skinned, about five feet four in height, thick as hell, and resembled Rihanna, so that was probably why she had so many niggas wanting to fuck with her.

After we were done eating, Bria and I split the bill before heading toward our car. She kissed me gently on my cheek before pulling away from me.

I stared into her hazel brown eyes and saw the pity in them. I looked away and began to play with my diamond ring.

"I hope you know what you doing, sis."

"I do," I mumbled before I watched her hop in her cream 2018 BMW X5 and pull off into the busy afternoon traffic.

As soon as I pulled back up at my job and stepped out, a bad feeling came over me. Every time I got one of those feelings, some shit always was about to pop off. I said a silent prayer before I clocked back in. Just as I had expected, I walked into a whole bunch of bullshit. It took everything I had to keep my cool when Jordan's ass had the nerve to lie on me to Mrs. Taylor. Those bitches were forever trying to make shit hard for me. Anytime some shit got fucked up, I was the first one that got blamed. Mrs. Taylor's hands were on her hips as she began to pop off the mouth about me not filling out the lunch chart properly on the time that the kids were fed lunch.

I swear, that woman was about to get smacked. The fact she kept pointing her finger at me like I was the problem was what really irked my nerves. I quickly closed my eyes and counted to five as I tried to calm myself down before I cursed that bitch out and dipped out on her ass.

"Mrs. Taylor, you told me to clock out and Jordan was supposed to be taking over. It was for her to fill out the rest of the lunch forms that I wasn't able to get to because you gave me an early lunch break."

Mrs. Taylor kept on talking shit, and I quickly rolled my eyes and ignored her ass.

"Do you know how bad I looked when Willie's dad came to pick him up, and Jordan handed him his lunch form only to find out that it was blank. Now, Willie's dad is jumping down my throat and making threats that he's going to report our center because he thinks we ain't feeding his child."

I wished this bitch would stop being so damn dramatic about every damn thing. I wanted to tell her some real shit, but I decided it was best to keep my mouth closed. If this center was more organized, if she hired a few more teachers, and if she stopped showing favoritism, a lot of this shit she was complaining about wouldn't even be happening. For the first time, I was happy when I began to smell poop. I dismissed myself out of Mrs. Taylor's presence as I went to change one of the kids. I sighed with relief when Mrs. Taylor left my damn room.

Today had been one of my kids' birthday, so I was doing everything in my power to make her day great. Jasmine was a wonderful baby and never gave me any problems. An hour later, I got a knock on my door, and a man who I'd never seen before stepped inside. I was down on the floor playing with the kids when I looked up and took him all in. He was sexy as hell, and he had my heart racing as he walked over to where I was sitting on the floor. He was as dark as a Hershey bar, tall as hell, and was rocking a neatly trimmed beard. I quickly got up off the floor and asked him his name and who he was coming to pick up.

"My name is Antwan, and I came to pick up my lil' godniece, Jasmine."

I sized him up, and my knees instantly grew week. I could tell by how this nigga was dressed and by his expensive jewelry that he was far from broke. His scent was intoxicating, and I found myself lusting after a nigga I knew nothing about. I looked away from him and headed toward my desk to make sure that he was on the list to pick up Jasmine. My palms began to sweat as I ran my finger down her checkout list until I found Antwan "Ace" Jenkins.

I grabbed Jasmine's papers that needed to be sent home and quickly grabbed Jasmine off the floor.

"Come here, sweetie. You about to go home." Jasmine started to try to whine, but when she saw who had come to pick her up, her whole demeanor changed. She clapped her small hands and cried out Ace's name.

"Hey, boo." Ace beamed as he picked Jasmine up and embraced her in a tight hug.

I had never seen Jasmine that happy to go home when her mom came to pick her up. Every time her mom came to pick her up, she was always whining and crying, but when her dad came to pick her up, she was always smiling and happy to go with him. I didn't know anything about her mom, but I did notice she always had some drama going on and was always on her phone cursing some bitch out. She was ghetto as hell. While Jasmine was sweet and calm, her mom was loud and had too much shit going on

61

for me, but that was just my opinion.

I placed a kiss on Jasmine's jaw before telling her happy birthday one last time. She smiled at me, and it melted my little heart.

"How did Jasmine act today?" Ace asked with concern.

"She was very good today. Jasmine is a sweetheart. I never have any problems with her."

Just when I thought Ace was about to leave, he turned around and tried to start a conversation with me.

"Excuse me, but what's your name?" Ace asked.

My heart skipped a beat because I couldn't believe that this nigga was actually trying to hold a conversation with me. I cleared my throat before I answered him.

"My name is Ms. Harmony."

"It's nice to meet you, Ms. Harmony."

Ace licked his juicy lips, and I swear, I almost literally fell over. I was in a trance, and the only thing that broke that trance was when I heard the kids crying for my attention.

Ace chuckled.

"Well, let me let you get back to work because your

kids look like they about to jump on me for stealing you away from them."

I laughed at him and blushed.

"Nice to meet you," I muttered before I turned back around so I could go back to giving my kids my full attention.

"Before I go, I wanted to know if I could get your number."

I froze because I knew if I gave this nigga my number, I was opening up a can of worms that didn't need to be opened. I bit down on my bottom lip as I closed my eyes then opened them with the urge to give him my number.

I slowly turned back around to him, and that's when he pointed at my big ass diamond rock on my finger.

"No disrespect to you or your man. If you don't feel comfortable giving me your number. I understand. I don't want no problems."

I rubbed my hands through my Remy weave and stared into his eyes. I heard myself spilling out my number and watched as he typed it into his iPhone. After he tapped save on his phone, Jordan's ass came into my room, trying to be nosy. She was staring at Ace like she wanted to rip the nigga's clothes off. I shook my head as he told me bye and left out the room. Jordan looked back at me and then toward the door where Ace had just left out of.

I could tell by how she was looking that she wanted to ask me what he and I were talking about, but instead, she told me that Mrs. Taylor wanted to see me in her office. The way she said that shit and how she looked put my ass on high alert. Something was about to go down, and I was clueless about what I was about to walk into.

"Okay cool. I will be back in a little bit," I mumbled to Jordan before I headed toward Mrs. Taylor's office.

I took my time as I walked my ass down the long hallway to her office. I knocked on her door once before she told me to come inside. Mrs. Taylor was a short Indian woman who looked to be in her early fifties. She had her glasses pushed on top of her head as she signaled for me to come in and have a seat. I closed the door behind me as I took a seat and waited for her to let a bitch know what was going on.

Mrs. Taylor cleared her throat and didn't show my ass

any mercy as she began to speak.

"Do you know why you are here?"

I looked at the bitch like she was crazy.

"After what happened with Willie, I think its best that we switch up your hours."

She pulled out a white piece of paper from her desk and handed it to me with my new schedule. I read the schedule to myself before I looked back at her trifling ass.

"You cut my hours?" I blurted out.

"I had no other choice. I feel like working ten-hour shifts every day is too much for you. You are starting to slack and forget the simplest things. It's best for you and everyone around here."

The bitch was lying through her teeth. She was making it seem like she was doing it for my best interest, but she was really doing it for her own reasons. I didn't even argue with the bitch. Instead, I got up and walked out her office.

# CHAPTER 5

## ROCCO

If my baby mama thought for one minute I was about to let her keep me from my daughter on her first birthday, then the bitch was crazy. If it wasn't for my nigga Ace, I didn't know what I would have done. London was acting crazy as hell, and I was getting sick of the shit. I noticed that every time that she and I weren't speaking, she always did some fuck shit to keep me away from my daughter.

She and I had fucked around less than six months before she got pregnant with Jasmine. London and I were never in a relationship, but she always tried to persuade me to make shit official with her, but I never wanted to.

London wasn't the type of bitch you wanted on your arm as your main bitch. She was a freak and always complained about how she had changed, but I knew she hadn't changed. She was down to fuck and suck anybody who was willing to throw her some cash. The way I met her was part of the reason why I felt I couldn't trust the hoe.

I had met London through my partner, Young G.

66

Young G had gone to high school with Ace and I back in the day, and we all were cool with one another. Just before Ace and I decided to say fuck school, Young G ended up moving from the Eastside to the Westside. When he moved to the Westside, he instantly started back slinging dope on the corner.

I always made sure to keep in touch with Young G because he was a cool ass nigga. Young G was a big-time dope dealer on the Westside, who was known for selling Molly and any other pill that you wanted to get high off of. His side hustle was shooting porn on the weekends, and that's when I first laid eyes on London's fine ass. Young G had chosen her as the main character in almost all of his flicks, and after first meeting her, I understood why. The bitch was bad as hell. I was instantly fascinated by her sexy ass. London was the complexion of mocha and resembled Kelly Rowland. She was thick in all the right places and knew how to suck a dick. She had a nigga instantly hooked, and I wasn't thinking about shit but getting my dick wet. One thing led to another, and I ended up fucking around and getting her ass pregnant. Even though I wasn't planning on making London a main fixture in my life, it ended up happening. She was just supposed to have been a good time, but I had fucked around and made the bitch a mother, and I was forever going to have to deal with her for Jasmine's sake.

I had just gotten back in town from taking care of some business with Young G and was on my way to pull up at Ace's spot to pick up my daughter when my phone began to blast Future. I groaned as I grabbed my phone off the passenger seat and noticed it was London calling my ass. I started not to pick up the phone but decided against it.

I placed my phone to my ear, and that's when London went in on my ass.

"Rocco, I told your ass good that you couldn't see Jasmine, but I see you still did what I told you not to."

"London, I don't give a fuck what you told me. Jasmine is my damn daughter, and I was not about to let your ass keep her away from me on her special day. I hate when your ass gets in your feelings because I swear you act like a little bitch."

"I wouldn't act like a bitch if you stop playing with my

emotions, nigga. You keep playing games with me, and I promise your ass I will be making a trip to your house."

"London, don't fucking play with me. You already knew before you started fucking with me that I had more than one bitch I was fucking around with. Don't act like you ain't know this shit."

"I don't give a fuck about none of them stinking pussy ass bitches. I got your baby, and I'm always going to be in your fucking face. When are you going to get this through your fucking head?"

I pulled the phone from my ear because I swear the bitch was delusional. She and I had nothing together and never would.

"London, get out your fucking feelings. All we do is fuck, and that's all we ever going to do. That's all we did way before you had Jasmine. Why you all of a sudden want to change your role?"

London became silent, and I pulled the phone away from my ear again to make sure she hadn't hung up.

Next thing I know, I hear her crying all in my ear. I had never heard London cry, so the shit took me by surprise, and I nearly ran into the car in front of me.

"London, you good, ma?" I asked her with concern in my voice.

"I've changed, Rocco. I'm more than just the bitch that you met on set at Young G spot. Can't you see that shit? I want more. I'm not a freak no more and ain't trying to be. Since I've had our daughter, I ain't even been featured in none of Young G's movies."

I became quiet as I listened to her tell me how much she had changed, and even though she sounded so convincing, I knew otherwise. Little did she know that I had someone watching her ass. She had been on watch since she pushed Jasmine out her pussy. I did it to keep my mind at peace and to make sure she was treating my daughter good when I wasn't around. I got a weekly report from a little nigga that I called Lil' Quan. He was currently in college and was trying to make some extra cash, so we set up a little deal. He got paid to watch my baby mama and to make sure she was taking care of my daughter. Every week, nothing had changed on the report. On the days that Jasmine was in school, I knew for a fact that

London was still being a little hoe. Even though she wasn't in the movies anymore, she was still sucking and fucking niggas just like the little freak that she was. Therefore, her sob story wasn't about to move me, and when she noticed she couldn't get me to respond like she wanted to, she quickly hung up on my ass.

I was forever relieved when the phone got quiet. I threw my phone back on the passenger seat, made a left, and pulled up at Ace's crib. Ace was living in a four-bedroom, five-bathroom house with a tennis court, a Jacuzzi out back along with a pool, and a big ass backyard where he would have parties. Ace and I were living good as hell there was no other nigga living better then us.

I hopped out my charcoal grey Porsche and knocked on his door. I waited for over five minutes before he brought his ass to the door. He was dressed in a pair of Nike basketball shorts, a Nike white shirt, and white and black Air Forces.

He dapped me up before he opened the door and let me in.

He already had Jasmine's bag packed and had her

ready to go. When she spotted me, she began making baby steps toward me. I picked her up and gave her some kisses on her cheek while I told her happy birthday in her ear. Jasmine was the best thing that ever happened to me, and I loved that little girl to death. I would fuck a nigga up about mine. Jasmine looked just like me and was rocking the same light-skinned complexion. When she got older, she was going to be breaking hearts.

"Nigga, I wanna know something."

"What you wanna know, nigga?" I asked Ace as I kissed my baby on her cheek.

"I went to pick up Jasmine, and bam, I laid my eyes on her teacher. Damn, she fine as hell, but I need you to be real with me, nigga... Have you tried fucking around with her?" Ace asked curiously.

I chuckled.

"Yeah, she fine and all, but I got one too many bitches on my plate to be adding anybody else to it, so I never tried fucking with her. Plus, she's my baby's teacher. I ain't about to get down like that."

Ace shook his head at me.

"Well, I'm glad your ass ain't tried her up because I'm going to make her mine."

I had never heard Ace talk like that about anybody, so I stared at his ass in amazement.

"Nigga, why you staring at me like that?" Ace asked.

"I'm trying to see who the fuck I'm talking to right about now because the Ace I know don't ever get in his feelings about a bitch."

"When I laid eyes on lil' mama today, I knew instantly she was different. She ain't like these nasty hoes around here. I want to get to know her, man."

"Well, all I can say is be careful, nigga."

"I always am, partna. What your plans for Jasmine's first birthday?" Ace asked curiously as he took a seat on his leather sectional.

"I got her some toys at the house that I bought her, but I ain't got no plans. I really just wanted to spend the day with her."

"Has London called your ass yet?"

"Hell yeah. She cursed me out."

Ace smirked.

"Nigga, you need to dead that shit with London. Bro, you gotta figure out if you gonna be with her or not because there is no way in hell she going to let you fuck other bitches if you giving her the dick too."

"Bro, I know what I'm doing. London ain't going to do shit. She going to play her position, or I will take Jasmine from her and cut her ass off."

Ace followed me out the house toward my Porsche. He was carrying over ten bags that were filled with toys and different outfits that he had bought Jasmine for her birthday.

"What time you want me to come through for Jasmine's party"

I checked my wrist and noticed it was almost six.

"She about to take her nap now, so I say come through about seven-thirty."

"Okay, nigga. See you then."

Ace and I dapped one another up before I dipped out.

As I drove home, I couldn't stop thinking about Ace and how much we had been through. Through it all, we had made it through the storm and were living the good life.

We were riding luxury cars, living in mansions, and were making boss moves. Niggas in Decatur knew never to try Ace or me. We had made a name in the streets and were known to murk a nigga if needed.

When I pulled up at my house, it was almost six thirty in the evening My plans were to chill the rest of the night, but when I pulled up to the front of my crib, I noticed London's black 2018 Jaguar that I purchased for her just a month earlier. A nigga had played it smart when I decided to not move a bitch in my crib, because London popping up would have my ass in a bad situation. I was heated as hell, but there was no way I was about to fuck around and fuss with London's crazy ass in front of my daughter. I looked in my rearview mirror and noticed Jasmine had fallen asleep.

London didn't even let my feet hit the ground before she walked over to me with her hands on her hips.

"What you want, London?"

"I came to see Jasmine. Today is her birthday. I think it's selfish that you want to keep her all damn day. I'm her mother, Rocco."

I closed my eyes as I counted to ten.

I opened them bitches, and London was still there staring at me. I knew that after our conversation, I was going to have to smoke me a fat ass blunt.

"London, don't be coming up in here starting shit with me. Jasmine back there in the seat sleep. Don't wake her up with that loud ass talking."

London became quiet.

Instead of entertaining her ass, I hopped out my whip and grabbed Jasmine out the back seat.

London followed me into the house and up the stairs to where Jasmine's room was neatly decorated with Disney's *Frozen* theme. I laid her down on her bed, kissed her on her cheek, and watched as London did the same. Jasmine normally took an hour nap, so while she was sleeping, I was going to use that time to set her party up.

When we made it downstairs, I headed toward the kitchen and pulled out Jasmine's small cake that she could smash with her hands.

My baby mama's eyes grew big when she noticed the cake and the toys that I had purchased for Jasmine's big day.

"I see you went all out," London admitted.

"Of course, I'm going to go all out. Today, our baby turns one."

When London's hands began to caress my back, my dick jumped. I wanted to pull away from her ass, but I just couldn't. All the frustration that I had been feeling outside had quickly evaporated. I looked down at her chocolate skin and was eager to get a taste of her sweetness. I took a step back when I heard Ace voice in my head about leaving London ass alone. It was time that I started to think with my brain and not with the head of my dick. There was no way I was about to break off any more dick to London I told myself. Rarely did we ever fuck, but when we did, shit got real very quickly.

London was dressed in a black top that squeezed her chocolate-hued titties together, a pair of denim booty shorts, and a pair of black flip-flops. She was looking sexy as hell, and the fact that she and I were alone wasn't making it any better. She licked her lips before taking my beer out my hand and placing it on the kitchen sink.

"Rocco, I'm not going anywhere, so I don't know why you always trying to fight the chemistry that you and I have for one another," she whispered in my ear before she began to work her hands down toward my belt buckle.

She didn't hesitate to get down on her knees and unbuckle my belt. I moaned as she pulled down my boxers and began to stroke on my rock-hard dick. One thing about London was she could suck a dick so good it would have your toes curling. She was just about to slide my dick into her mouth when my phone began to blast Travis Scott's "Goosebumps." My heart stopped because that was the ringtone for another one of my hoes that I was fucking with. I tried pushing London away, but she wasn't budging. Instead, she slid my dick into her mouth and started sucking.

Instead of ignoring the call, I picked up my phone and acted calm and cool, even though London was on her knees giving me some sloppy head.

"Hey, bae. What are you doing?"

"I'm up here just chilling and getting ready to celebrate my daughter's birthday party."

"Okay. Well, did you want me to stay the night?"

I looked down at London and closed my eyes as I tried to decide if I wanted her to stay the night or not.

When London began to suck on my balls, I nearly moaned into the phone, and I had to catch myself.

"Nah, boo. You ain't got to stay the night. I got to get up early in the morning to take care of some business."

I could hear the disappointment in her voice, and I quickly tried to dead it before it got out of control.

"I will come over as soon as I take care of my business in the morning."

I hurried her off the phone because the whole time I was talking to her, I was holding my nut. After I ended the call, I gripped London's hair and began to slide in and out of her until I busted all my warm cream into her mouth.

London pulled away from me, ran to the kitchen sink, and emptied her mouth. She looked back at me with anger in her eyes.

"I swear, you need to leave them other bitches alone. Why the fuck are you with them anyway, Rocco?"

I didn't respond at first because I wasn't about to

entertain London. As I zipped up my shorts and began to fix my clothes, London's words began to haunt me. Getting my dick sucked was a requirement to be with me, and the fact that a few of the bitches I was fucking with didn't do half the shit that I liked was the real reason I always kept London close by me. She always knew how to please me.

Don't get me wrong, I fucked on the regular, but none of those hoes could set my body on fire like my baby mama. London knew what she was doing, and she was always anxious to please a nigga. That was one of the main reasons why I always tried to look out for her.

I didn't mind giving London money to pay her bills, and I always gave her money to buy anything her heart desired when she wasn't acting crazy as hell. I mean, I'd rather give it to her than for her to be spreading her legs open on them porn flicks for some money. London didn't have to stress about shit, but yet and still, she wasn't satisfied. She had everything her heart desired, but when I looked into her eyes, I could tell that she was still unhappy.

"London, I give you everything that you ask me to give

you, and still, your ass finds something you ain't happy about. What more do you want me to do?"

Her eyes sparkled as she walked over to where I was standing. She placed her finger over my lips before whispering in my ear, "I want you. I'm tired of sharing you with all them other hoes."

She pulled away from me, and neither one of us spoke for the longest time. Just when I was about to speak, I heard Jasmine crying upstairs.

I could tell that yet again, I didn't tell London what she wanted to hear because she rolled her eyes at me and headed upstairs to check on Jasmine.

# CHAPTER 6

# HARMONY

*I closed my eyes as he began to lick and suck on my neck. I moaned when he flicked his tongue over each nipple just before he started to suck gently on each one. My pussy tingled, and I was craving him.*

*"I want you," I whispered.*

*"How bad do you want me?" he asked.*

*I wanted to speak, but no words were able to come from my mouth.*

*He chuckled just before he placed his head between my legs and began to lightly suck on my clit. I gripped the sheets as he began to eat my pussy like it was his last meal.*

*When he slid a finger inside my wetness and flicked his tongue over my sensitive clit, I was ready to cum right then and there.*

*"Ace," I cried out as my body began to shake.*

*I shut my eyes tightly as my juices spilled from my body.*

*Ace gripped my hips firmly as he gladly slurped up my juices.*

When I opened my eyes, I groaned. Sex with Ace had been a dream, and I was disappointed. The dream I had just woken up from had been a dream that I hated had ended. I pulled the covers over my face and was about to go back to sleep only for them to be yanked from my body a few moments later.

"Baby, get up. It's Saturday, and I cooked you breakfast."

The smell of bacon filled the bedroom. My stomach began to growl as I sat up in bed. I was amazed to find that Kannon was shirtless and was holding my breakfast tray in his hands. It had been only two weeks since Kannon had proposed to me, and since that day, I had seen a dramatic change with him. He was treating me like the queen that I was. I couldn't remember the last time Kannon had done anything so romantic before in my life. He placed a kiss on my cheek before he handed me my tray and headed toward the bathroom to take a shower. I ate my bacon, eggs, and toast and sipped on my steaming hot Starbucks coffee that he had brewed for me. As I ate my food, I instantly began to feel guilty for dreaming about fucking another nigga that wasn't my man. Even though I was with Kannon and he had my heart, I couldn't erase meeting Ace and the feelings that I had when I met him. Ace was sexy as hell, and I secretly was lusting after his ass. The fact that he hadn't yet called me gave me the first sign that he probably wasn't interested in me anyway. My heart sort of sunk because I had no clue if he and I were ever going to see each other again. I quickly pushed Ace out of my mind and decided to finish eating my food.

After I was done eating, Kannon came back in the room with a grey towel wrapped around his waist.

He was looking sexy as hell, and he had my pussy craving some affection. He smirked when he noticed me staring at him.

"Come here, baby. You know if you want this dick, you can take it. You ain't got to stare me down."

I was horny as hell because it had been almost four months since Kannon and I had even fucked. After, I found out about him cheating on me with the neighbor, I surely didn't want him touching me. The fact that he had kept his emotions in check and was treating me with respect, I felt

84

like it was okay to give him a little sample of the pussy. When his lips met mine, I felt as if I was in heaven. Our tongues danced with one another as he slid his fingers through my weave. He caressed my neck as he slid his tongue down my throat. I moaned as I begged him to take his towel off and break me off a little of his dick.

Just when he was about to stick me, my phone began to ring. I groaned and wasn't going to answer it but changed my mind, thinking that I could be important. I picked up when I noticed that it was Bria calling me. Kannon didn't stop what he was doing. Instead, he started sucking on my neck which had a bitch ready to fuck and give him the pussy.

I moaned softly into the phone as Bria yelled out my name.

I could hear the urgency in Bria's voice, and I quickly pushed Kannon off of me and gave my full attention to Bria.

"What's wrong, Bria?"

"Boo, you need to come to the shop. We need to talk about some important shit."

I looked over at Kannon, who looked to be irritated but when he saw me staring he quickly looked away and started getting dressed for the day.

"I will be there in fifteen minutes," I muttered into the phone before disconnecting the call.

"What your girl wanted?" Kannon asked as I headed toward the bathroom, so I could take a shower.

"I really don't know," I replied truthfully.

Kannon walked over to me and placed his hand on my cheek before giving me a kiss on my lips.

"I just want you to know that I love you, baby. Always remember that."

"I will," I choked out as I stared into his eyes.

I hopped in the shower, and as the water began to caress my body, I began to wonder what Bria had to tell me that was so urgent that she couldn't tell me over the phone.

My thoughts were interrupted when I heard Kannon calling out my name.

"Baby, I'm about to head out with Young G for a quick minute. We got to make some moves. Don't wait up for me tonight!" Kannon yelled out from the bedroom.

"Okay, baby!" I yelled back as I continued to rub my body with my favorite Dove soap.

There had been a time that I hated when Kannon used to fuck with Young G, but eventually I learned to tolerate his ass. Young G kept Kannon heavy in the streets, but I learned to get out my feelings about the shit because Kannon was making major moves and was bringing home a lot of money whenever Young G came around. The only reason why I didn't too much care for Young G was because I felt like he was part of the reason that Kannon had started fucking around on me. I knew that sounded stupid as hell, but Young G was always trying to get Kannon to talk to other bitches behind my back, and I had a problem with that shit. Kannon had no clue that I had been eavesdropping on some of their conversations when Young G would bring his ass over to the house late at night. I never bothered with confronting Kannon because I knew that was only going to lead to an argument that I wasn't going to win.

After I was done showering, I stepped out and dried off

my wet body. I grabbed my iPhone so I could check the weather for that day. It was close to eighty degrees outside, so I decided to wear something that I wouldn't be hot in. After I had picked out my clothes for that day, I made sure to lotion my body down and began to get dressed. I applied a small amount of makeup, eyeliner, mascara, and a little eyeshadow before I started flat ironing my weave.

When I stared at myself in the mirror and liked what I saw. My caramel complexion was glowing again. At one point in time, I was looking pale and sick, but now, I looked healthier because I wasn't as depressed like I was in the previous months. I was slim but had a small booty that hugged my white shorts. I took a few pictures and posted them on the 'Gram before I grabbed my keys and headed out the house.

Traffic was light, and it didn't take me any longer than fifteen minutes to pull up at Bria's hair salon. Bria was making major moves. Going to get her license to do hair was the best shit Bria could have done. Since I had known Bria back in high school, she always had been good at doing hair. So, when I went to college for an education, she went to get her license for hair. She first started doing hair out her home, but next thing you know, Tay took it upon himself to take her further and purchased her a shop. Since she had opened her salon, she was now pulling in so much money that Bria didn't really have to ask Tay for shit. She was independent, and I was happy for her ass.

I pulled up next to Bria's BMW, slid on my Gucci shades, and headed inside the salon. When I stepped inside, all eyes were on me. I was just about to head to the back toward Bria's office, but the girl that was up front stopped me. I looked down at her name tag and noticed that her name was Claudia.

When our eyes connected, I could tell instantly that the bitch had an issue with me. One thing I hated about these hoes was they always showed signs of jealousy when they first laid eyes on me. Any bitch who came in contact with me either liked me or didn't, and from how this bitch was looking at me, I could tell she disliked my ass.

"I'm Harmony, Bria's best friend. She's expecting me," I told the girl with just as much attitude that she was showing me.

She rolled her eyes at me, which made me want to jump across the table and punch her right in the throat. Claudia was just about to say some slick shit when Bria came out of her office. When Bria told Claudia to let me through, the look on Claudia's face was priceless.

Bria was dressed in a yellow sundress and was rocking a pair of Gucci flip-flops.

"Bitch, you seriously need to hire better staff. Claudia was about to get her throat punched with all them hateful stares she was giving me. She act like she got a problem or some shit."

Bria laughed.

"Claudia just in her feelings because I threatened to fire her ass if she continues to be late. It's nothing personal against you, sis. I would have been canned her ass, but I'm trying my best not to be such a bitch these days."

"Bitch, please. That's your makeup; you can't change that shit," I joked Bria.

Bria laughed as we headed into her office.

"What you up to?" I asked her as I took a seat.

"Trying to get payroll done. Everyone gets paid

tomorrow."

I eyed her up because I could tell how she was looking that something was bothering her.

"Bria, what was so important that you had me get out my bed and miss the morning dick that Kannon was trying to give me?"

Bria's face twitched up like she had just eaten something sour.

"What the fuck wrong with you?" I asked her.

"When I tell you what I'm about to tell you, you going to be glad he didn't give you no morning dick."

My heart felt as if it was about to fall out my chest. My palms began to sweat as I began to fidget in my seat. I closed my eyes and said a silent prayer that whatever that Bria was about to tell me wasn't true.

"Today, some bitch by the name of Torri came in to get her hair retwisted."

"Hold the fuck up. Describe the bitch for me."

"She medium height, she light-skinned, got a fat ass, but her chest flat as hell, and she rocking some twists in her head that's dyed like a burgundy."

After she described the bitch, I was heated than a motherfucka.

"That's the bitch who lives up the road from me. She's the one he cheated on me with."

Bria looked like she wanted to throw up.

"Kannon is nasty as fuck for that shit. The bitch ain't even cute. But anyway, she came with her homegirl. I was in the front trying to make sure everybody had signed in to get their hair done, and that's when I overheard Torri tell the bitch who she was with that she had been fucking with some nigga by the name of Kannon…"

"Kannon still fucking that bitch?" I asked angrily.

"Baby, him fucking her still isn't your concern. I think you need to get tested because ole girl was heated as hell. She started talking about how Kannon gave her genital herpes and gonorrhea. After she confronted him on the shit, he started ignoring her calls and text messages."

My mouth dropped open, but no words came out. I couldn't speak; I was speechless. I couldn't believe that the nigga I was soon going to marry had possibly contracted herpes and gonorrhea. My pussy began to tingle and not in a good way because I had no clue if he had passed me that shit.

"Harmony, are you okay?" Bria asked with concern on her face.

Tears welled up in my eyes, and I couldn't hold it back. I felt so betrayed because this nigga had not only cheated on me, but his ass had possibly given me some shit. Bria walked over to me and held me as I cried my eyes out.

I pulled away from Bria and wiped the tears from my eyes.

"You just don't know how bad I want to fuck Kannon's ass up right about now. The fact this nigga gonna propose to me like he had changed only to be still smashing these hoes makes me want to hurt his ass right about now. If I wasn't scared of going to prison, I would seriously put his ass six feet deep.

"Bitch, let me take care of Kannon. I have been wanting to murk his ass after he laid hands on your ass the first time."

I shook my head, and Bria sighed with frustration.

"I don't know what you love about this nigga, and why

you always trying to save his ass. When will you learn that Kannon can't be trusted, boo? He ain't shit, and you keep on taking him back and forgiving him only going to make shit worse. Now that you know he still fucking around with not only the bitch up the street but possibly other hoes, what are you going to do with this information?"

I licked my lips and looked down at the diamond ring that I was rocking on my left finger. All that shit had been a lie. He was still up to his same old tricks, and I wanted no part of the bullshit. For the first time, I felt something wash over me, and something clicked inside my heart that enough was enough. It was time to get away from Kannon. If I didn't, he was going to continue to hurt me. Love wasn't supposed to hurt, but he was literally murdering my ass by stabbing me in my already half-broken heart.

"If I leave, where am I going to go? My job ain't hitting on shit. I can't even afford an apartment on my own. Everything I have is what Kannon gave me."

"Bitch, don't sit here and tell me this sob story about you don't have anywhere to go. You can come stay with me. Tay won't mind. I'm living in a damn three-bedroom, three-bathroom home. I got more than enough room for you. My house is big enough for you to have your own shit. You can stay as long as you want, boo. But please get the fuck away from Kannon, and if I was you, I would go and get checked out just in case."

"But I haven't had any symptoms of no STD. It's been a while since him and I have actually fucked."

"That shit don't matter, boo. You still could have been exposed to the STD's. Just go get checked out. Better safe than sorry. I love you like a sister. If you don't have anyone else, you got me. I know you hate to give up that lifestyle, but it's gonna be worth it, sis. You going to feel free again."

I listened to everything that she was saying, but I was ready to get off the topic and talk about something else. I was hurting like crazy, and all I wanted to do was go home and cry into my pillow until I figured out what was going to be my next move. I quickly changed the topic and began telling her about the nigga that I had met at work named Ace. As I described who the nigga was, how fine he looked, Bria wanted to know if I got his number, but I quickly shook my head and told her that I had given him my number instead.

"To be honest, Bria, I don't know if he even going to call. I got so much shit going on right now that fucking around on Kannon isn't about to happen. I just need to take a break from all men if Kannon and I don't work out."

Bria rolled her eyes.

"Harmony, listen to yourself you talking some crazy shit right about now. Just because Kannon is a whack ass motherfucka don't mean every nigga on this planet gonna be that way. See, this nigga Ace may be different. I think you need to give him a try if he contacts you."

I agreed, and we talked for a little while longer before I hurried out her office. When I hopped in my car, I checked the time and noticed it was only two in the afternoon. I quickly pulled into the intersection and headed straight to Urgent Care so I could get checked out. There was no way I was about to go home and mope around after Bria had told me about the STD's. I wanted to hurry and get myself checked out, so I could put my mind at rest. When I pulled up at the clinic, I hopped out my car and hurried inside. After I had signed myself in, I filled out some paperwork since it was my first time coming and waited to be called in the back. I waited almost an hour before my name was called. I grabbed my Louis Vuitton bag and followed the nurse toward the back. The nurse introduced herself as Amy. She was medium height, with long blonde hair that she had pulled up in a bun. When she asked me why I was there, I began to fidget in my seat. I felt embarrassed as hell and wanted to disappear when she eyed me and waited for me to answer her question.

"I think I've been exposed to gonorrhea and genital herpes."

The nurse began to write something down in my chart and began the process of checking me out.

"Have you had any symptoms of burning, weird discharge, pain, itching, etcetera?"

"No," I muttered.

"Okay. I tell you what... I will give you an STD test, and we will go from there."

I nodded my head and waited until she got back. When she came back with a small cup, I grabbed it and went to go fill it with pee. After I was done, I headed back to the room and took a seat. A few moments later, she came in the room, took a blood sample, and told me she would have my results in twenty-four hours.

I thanked her and left out the office. All the way home I was praying that everything came back negative. I didn't want to live with herpes for the rest of my life. I was hot and angry as hell, but I knew I had to get my emotions in check because there was no way I was ready to address Kannon with the information that I had found out.

"What happens if the bitch was lying?" I asked myself.

I pulled up at my house twenty minutes later and hopped out. I was grateful that Kannon wasn't home just yet. I needed to calm myself down before he brought his ass home later that night.

I headed straight to the kitchen and poured me a glass of wine as I took a seat in the living room couch. What if I had both STD's it, what was my life going to be like? I was in such a deep thought that when my phone started to vibrate it jolted me from the horrible things that was racing in my head. I grabbed my phone, but when I noticed that it was Bria I quickly threw my phone back on the couch. I wasn't mad at her, but at the moment I wanted to think and get my thoughts right before I talked to anyone.

After my third glass of wine I stood up to cut on me some music. My knees and legs felt wobbly, but I did manage to cut on my surround sound without falling down. As I took a seat back on my couch and as Travis Scott blasted from my speakers, all the stress from that day finally took it tole on me. A few moments later I closed my eyes and that's when sleep came for me.


It was around eleven when Kannon decided to bring his ass home. I could smell weed and liquor before he even made his way over to me. I cringed when he came over to where I was sitting on the couch. My head was aching me but through all the pain I still wanted to know. I needed to know to put my mind at ease if Kannon was infected and if he was still cheating on me with other hoes? Hot tears stung my eyes, but I didn't dare let Kannon see them.

"Baby," he mumbled just before he placed a kiss on my ear.

That nigga was high as hell and was ready to fuck I could heard it in his voice. When his hands began to play with my titties, I was screaming out in my head for him to stop. There was no way I was about to fuck that nigga if I had suspicions of him having that shit.

I was grateful when his phone began to ring, and he pulled away from me. I turned around and noticed his face twitched up in anger. I didn't know who had texted him, but it had him all in his feelings.

I was just about to ask him what was wrong with his ass when a loud knock came at the door. I had no clue who could be knocking at the door this damn late. I eyed Kannon up but he wouldn't make direct eye contact with me. Kannon rarely brought anyone over, and rarely did anyone come to visit. I was about to head to the door when Kannon grabbed me by the arm.

"Go back and sit down, baby. I will see who at the door."

The once high Kannon looked sober as hell at that very moment. There was no way I was about to sit my ass down anywhere. His ass was acting way too suspicious for me.

Something was up, and I was about to find out what it was.

My heart wasn't ready when Kannon opened that door, and I spotted Torri's bitch ass standing on my step.

"What the fuck are you doing here?" Kannon asked angrily.

Torri was dressed in a pair of ripped skinny jeans, a white top, and a pair of all white Jordan's. Her hair was freshly twisted, and the scent of her Chanel perfume filled the air. She didn't even respond to Kannon. Instead, she pushed her way into the house. She placed her hands on her hips before she began to give Kannon the business.

"Nigga, I been blowing up your phone all damn week. You think you can ignore me? Nigga, your nasty dick ass gave me herpes. What makes you think I'm just going to up and disappear just because you ignoring me, nigga? No, boo, what I need for you to do is run me my money, so I can continue to take my fucking medicine?" Torri yelled at Kannon.

Kannon's face was screwed up in anger, and he looked like he was about to choke Torri's ass out. If I were her, I would have dipped out quickly, but that bitch had a lot of shit to get off her chest.

When Torri's eyes locked with mine, I knew instantly she was about to spit some real shit at me.

"I think it's time for you to know the truth about your nigga. Kannon and I been fucking around for a quick minute. I'm going to be real with your ass. This nigga ain't never been faithful to your ass. I think it's time for you to stop walking around Decatur like your nigga just the shit because he's not. Your nigga is out here in these streets slanging dick to anybody who willing to give him the pussy and lets not forget he spreading herpes and all other types of STD's. If you ain't been tested, I would be if I was you."

Before I could even respond, Kannon had grabbed Torri by her throat and began choking her ass out. I stood there horrified as I watched the scene play out. He hissed something in her ear and then dropped her ass on the floor.

Tears ran down her cheeks as she coughed and gasped for air. She looked up at me like I was about to help her ass up. She was sadly mistaken if she thought I was about to help her out. She finally got her ass off the hardwood floor while holding her hand to her throat.

"You won't ever have to worry about me fucking your dirty dick ever again," she hissed at Kannon before she dipped out.

Just before she was about to go, she looked back at me and spoke some real shit.

"If your tests come back clean, then, bitch, you lucky."

"Get the fuck out my house, bitch!" Kannon screamed before he slammed the door in Torri's face.

My mouth stood open when Kannon looked over at me. His veins were popping out his head, and his fists were balled up.

He walked over to me, and I took a few steps back. I hated that she had even brought her ass over here and pissed him off. Little did she know that word had already gotten back to me that Kannon was passing out STD's. I was even more eager to get my test results back because I wanted to know the truth. *Did Kannon give her that shit, or was she slutting around and got it from some other random nigga? If Kannon did give her that shit, who else had he been fucking around with?* I thought to myself.

"Baby, whatever you do, don't listen to that hoe. I know I fucked up by fucking around with her ass, but I don't got shit. My dick is clean. I put my life on that shit. If she got anything, it's probably from some of them niggas she was fucking around with. Every time I smashed her ass, I wrapped up."

I looked into Kannon's eyes, but something was telling me that this nigga was lying through his teeth. But what I found strange was if he actually had herpes or gonorrhea, wouldn't I have seen some type of medicine? I never saw him take shit besides a pain reliever. I looked at his ass and shook my head because something just wasn't right about any of this. I didn't know who to leave a nasty hoe or the nigga who claimed he loved me. Instead of fighting with his ass, I headed upstairs so I could get ready for work the next morning.

# CHAPTER 6

## ACE

"Baby, where you going?" Crystal asked gently just before I slid out of bed.

"I got some business to take care of," I mumbled as I searched for my clothes and shoes. As I was dressing, I noticed Crystal watching me. I could tell by how she was looking that she was about to say some dumb shit. I hated that I had been weak as hell and had even brought my ass over to her house late last night. My body was screaming for some type of release, and Crystal had given me that shit.

I closed my eyes as I thought back to the amazing head that she had performed on me the night before. She had a nigga's toes curling. That was just how good it was.

"Baby, why are you acting so distant toward me? We have been talking for a while now. I thought by now you would be ready to settle down and give me your heart. I've fallen in love with you," Crystal admitted.

My body began to become tense when she walked over to where I was dressing and placed her hands on my back.

I pulled away from her, glared at her half-naked body, and then stared into her eyes.

"Crystal, I told you when we first started kicking it that I wasn't looking for love and to not fall in love with me, but apparently, you didn't listen to me."

I noticed the tears that were falling from Crystal's eyes, but I didn't let that shit change how I was feeling at the moment. She had fucked around and had gotten her feelings involved, and there was nothing that I could do to fix the shit. I placed a kiss on her cheek and told her I was about to go.

"Fuck you, Ace. Just forget all this shit. If I can't have your heart, then I don't want nothing from your ass."

I knew shorty was lying and was trying to play the victim role, but like I said earlier, I knew a gold digger when I saw one, and she was a fucking gold digger who loved to try to hide who she really was. To shut her ass up, I pulled out two stacks from my cargo shorts and handed it to her.

She quickly got quiet before staring up at me with her

big pretty eyes. She pushed her curly weave from her face before she wiped the last of her tears from her eyes. I didn't even give her ass time to respond before I dipped out on her ass.

I headed home in a daze because I had a lot of shit going on in my personal life. With my uncle fighting for his life and me getting my paper, my plate was full. I had just pulled up at my house when Harmony crossed my mind. Meeting her at the daycare had done something to my ass. It was something about her that gave me the vibe that she was different. I wanted her, but at the same time, the fact she had someone was what really kept me from going after her. Even though I was raised in the streets and was a certified street nigga, I refrained from fucking with bitches who already had a nigga. I wasn't the type of nigga to beef with niggas over a bitch, and I didn't have time to have to murk a nigga because he was in his feelings because his bitch wanted to fuck with me.

Normally, I was always a good judge of people when I first met them, so I knew Harmony had to have been different because I didn't get a bad vibe from her. No one

107

was perfect, but she seemed perfect from what I had seen from just the ten minutes of being in her presence. I was just about to head in the house and take me a shower when Rocco hit my line up and told me about these niggas that he was thinking about doing business with. Rocco and I had been in the streets for a very long time, but when it comes to looking for connects, I always was very cautious of fucking around with niggas who I didn't know shit about.

"Who told you about these niggas?" I asked Rocco suspiciously.

"Young G told me about these niggas. He already introduced me to them."

I was on high alert anytime I heard this nigga say anything about Young G. Word on the street was that Young G was working with the FEDs, but I had no clue how true that shit was. If a nigga was caught snitching, he would be dead, and Young G was still breathing... at least for now. Something was up with Young G, and there was no way I wanted anything to do with him period. Even though all of us had gone to high school together, Young

G was more Rocco's friend than mine. Even back when we were kids, I noticed his ass was always hating, but Rocco always claimed I was imagining shit.

"Rocco, I want to know why in the hell are you going with Young G to go meet some niggas when I'm your partna? When the fuck you went to meet these niggas?" I asked angrily.

"I went to meet them on the day you went to pick Jasmine up from school."

"Nigga, you told me you were going to the doctor."

"I lied, bro. Don't be mad, damn. I wasn't trying to do any of this shit to keep you out the loop, but look, bro, I ain't tell you because I wanted to make sure they weren't on no bullshit. Plus, I know how you feel about Young G I didn't want to tell you that he knew these niggas. If I would have told you that Young G had hooked me up there was no way you was going to come along anyway. I know you don't like Young G for whatever reason, but I'm telling you, this shit looks like a good deal. These niggas that Young G know, they have that real shit with better quality. It's way more money than what we making now."

I sighed with frustration because Rocco was money hungry and didn't care about shit else.

"Rocco, listen to me. Don't do that shit. I don't want to have shit to do with Young G and anybody he knows. That nigga ain't about shit, and you need to get that shit through your head."

I was just about to say more, but Rocco told me he had another call, and he would hit me back later. I shook my head, stepped out my car, and headed in the house.

The whole time I showered, I couldn't stop thinking about Rocco and what he had told me over the phone. I prayed that nigga didn't try to get himself mixed in with Young G. Because if he was snitching, this would end badly for Rocco and me. Never had Rocco and I ever made any decisions without one another, but after he had gone behind my back and had basically met with those niggas, I felt some type of way.

If Rocco wanted to do this shit by himself, then he could. I was going to continue to fuck with Young Scooter because I knew his ass wasn't going to fuck me over. If Rocco was smart, he would do the same.

\*\*\*\*\*\*\*\*\*\*

I pulled up at the hospital so I could check in on my uncle. I felt sort of guilty because I had been so busy with my life that I had neglected my uncle for nearly two days. I took a seat next to his bed and watched him as his chest rose up and down as he snored loudly. I didn't want to wake him, so I decided to sit there and chill out until he opened his eyes. I had spoken to his nurse about his health, and when they told me that he was getting worse, my heart broke. My uncle had always been a fighter, and I hated that it was probably going to be the last battle that he was going to have to fight before he was called home.

An hour later, my uncle opened his eyes and smiled at me.

"Ace, is that you, son?" Uncle Dro asked.

"Yeah, it's me. Sorry I ain't been by. A lot of shit been going on that I couldn't get away."

When my uncle started coughing, I passed him some water, but he turned it down. He grabbed my hand and pulled me closer to him.

"I'm so glad that you came today. I have something to tell you that I was meaning to tell you a few days ago."

"What you got to tell me?" I asked him emotionally.

"Before Rabbit was murdered, he left you some money, but he made me promise not to give it to you or tell you unless you really needed it. The money he gave you in that duffle bag that night wasn't nearly half of what he got from robbing them New Orleans niggas. He hid over half a million for you, and it was for me to watch over until I felt like you were ready to get it. Now that I'm about to die, I think it's time to tell you about it."

I was speechless because I was not expecting for Uncle Dro to tell me some shit like that.

"I got everything set up in an off-shore account with your name on it. Nobody can touch that money but you. I have the information that you need at the house. What I need for you to do is go home, look in the safe in my office, and you will find all the information that you need."

I was stunned.

"You kept that much money this long for me?" I asked emotionally.

"Of course, I did. There was no way I was about to spend any of your money. Rabbit gave that money to you. I wouldn't do no shit like that to you, son. I love you like you are my own."

The fact that my uncle could have fucked me over and spent that money years ago let me knew that he had nothing but loyalty toward my father and me. My mind was running a mile a minute, but it quickly came to a halt when he told me he was worried about Rocco.

"What you mean, Uncle Dro?"

"Something up with that boy? Normally, I go to sleep every night and never dream, but the past two nights, I've dreamed of seeing Rocco being murdered. The dream is so horrifying that I wake up in  cold sweats. Ace, Rocco is lost, and I'm worried. If he don't get himself out of the streets, he going to end up dead. I can't die knowing Rocco is out here doing Lord knows what in these streets. Ace, you have always been smart as hell about shit, and you always think shit through, but Rocco is so impulsive and doesn't see shit for what it is. He's money hungry, and him being that way will fuck him up in the long run. I have enough money for you and him both to live off of when I die. Everything I own is in that safe I was telling you about in my office. All you need is the code to get inside."

"Uncle Dro, don't be saying shit like that. You going to be okay."

Uncle Dro shook his head.

"Ace, all I ask of you is to make sure you look out for Rocco. I know he hardheaded, but do what you can to keep him out of harm's way. I already know my time is coming to an end. I just want you to know that I got enough money hid so that you and Rocco will never have to hustle on the block ever again. Take the money, invest it, and spend it wisely. I have faith that you are going to look out for Rocco. You always have."

I pulled my phone out my pocket and typed in the code that my uncle gave me. I was just about to slide the phone back in my pocket when he grabbed me by my hand.

"Thanks, Uncle Dro," I choked out before I leaned in and gave him a hug.

*******

I couldn't stop thinking about the conversation that

Uncle Dro and I shared the day before. My heart was heavy because I hated thinking that the only man that I knew was soon going to die. I wanted nothing more than to hit Rocco up, but I decided against it. I wasn't in the mood to deal with Rocco at the moment. All I wanted to do was chill, but I had no one that I felt like chilling with. Calling Crystal was out of the question. After I had given her those two stacks, I had erased her number out my phone and had even blocked her ass so she couldn't reach me. I wanted Crystal out of my life. I wanted any gold digging bitch that I had fucked with out of my life as well. Today, my plans were to hit the gym and clean out my phone from all the hoes that I had smashed. It was time for a new me. I wanted more than someone to fuck; I wanted something that was going to last a lifetime. Fucking around with those hoes, I wasn't getting anywhere near meeting the woman of my dreams.

I hit the gym up and worked my ass off until I was sweaty and tired. I sipped on a bottle of water as I watched the rest of gym members work out. After I had rested up, I grabbed my duffle bag and headed out toward my car. The wind was strong as ever but felt cold on my wet skin. I wiped my brow as I unlocked my car and stepped inside my Aston Martin. I was just about to pull off when my phone started ringing. When I noticed it was Rocco, I immediately picked up.

"Bro, you good?" I asked Rocco.

I couldn't hear anything but Rocco crying into my ear.

"Bro, what's going on?" I asked with panic in my voice.

"Dad is gone, man. He just passed away."

Tears fell from my eyes because the day had finally come that Uncle Dro was no longer going to suffer. I quickly disconnected the call as I wiped the tears that had fallen down my cheeks. I closed my eyes as I said a silent prayer that Uncle Dro was in a better place.

## **FOUR DAYS LATER**

It had been four days since my uncle had passed, and I still was in utter shock about the news. Yes, my uncle was sick, but I never thought that he would have given up the fight like he had. I could still remember the last talk that he

116

and I shared before he died. Tears began to fall from my eyes as I thought back on how he begged me to look after Rocco and to keep him safe. I just prayed that I didn't disappoint him.

"Uncle Dro, I know you up in heaven looking down at me. Please, help me get through today," I mumbled.

A few moments later, I heard a loud knock at my front door. I already knew it was probably Rocco, letting me know that he was about to head over to the church. I was dressed in all black and was rocking bags under my eyes because I hadn't slept in days. I hurried down the stairs and opened the door to find Rocco looking similar to me. He was dressed in all black while his long dreads were pulled back from his face in a ponytail, and he was also rocking bags under his eyes. His eyes were bloodshot red, so I figured that he had probably had been crying.

He slid his Gucci shades over his eyes before dapping me up. I followed him outside and hopped in his gray Porsche with him. I stared out the window and noticed that the skies were dark, and it was very cloudy. I figured that it was going to rain but I only prayed it didn't start until after Uncle Dro was in the ground. We sped down the road until we pulled up at First Baptist Church. It was the church that Uncle Dro started going to when he was first diagnosed with lung cancer.

The church was so packed that people had to park on the side of the roads. I was glad that Rocco and I had reserved our own spot at the front door. He and I didn't bother taking a limousine because Uncle Dro didn't have any family. We were all he had. Everyone else was just niggas he had been raised with and had been fucking around with on the streets heavily when he was slinging dope on the corner. Everyone was just coming to show respect for my uncle and say their final goodbyes. From the time we stepped inside the church, all eyes were on me and Rocco. We nodded our heads as we headed toward the front and took a seat. The whole funeral was sad as fuck. Rocco tried to be tough, but I could tell that he wanted to cry. When it was time to view the body, Rocco was the first one in the front of the line.

I watched as Rocco wiped his tears and placed a kiss on his father's cheek. I also did the same and watched as the whole church said their goodbyes. When the preacher asked if anyone wanted to come up and speak about my uncle, nobody stood up. Everyone was way too emotional to mumble one word. I looked over at Rocco, and I knew instantly that he wasn't going to be able to say anything. As I walked up toward the front, all the gangsters young and old, watched me as I began to speak about Uncle Dro. I could hear babies crying and women sobbing, but I knew I had to get the shit off my chest.

"My uncle was an amazing man. We had always been close growing up, but when my father was taken away from me, my uncle never once abandoned me. He took care of me and raised me up to be the man that I am today. Even though I wasn't his biological son, he treated me no differently than he treated Rocco. I have nothing but respect and love for him."

Tears fell from my eyes as I began to have flashbacks of when I was growing up with Rocco. I had gotten so emotional over the speech that I couldn't continue to say what I felt was needed to be said. The pastor walked over to me and tried to console me. After the pastor gave me a hug, he whispered some inspirational words in my ear.

I took my seat next to Rocco and wiped my eyes as the pastor began to preach about Uncle Dro and all the great things he had done for the community when he got older. After the funeral was over, everyone walked over to Rocco and I to tell us how sorry they were for our loss. I didn't know how I managed to get through the funeral, but I knew it had to be the man above who got me through it. When it was time to place my uncle in the ground, the sky opened up, and the rain began to come down hard as hell. I held my umbrella tightly as the wind began to blow harder.

I listened as the preacher began to shout, "For dust thou art, and unto dust shalt thou return!"

My heart broke into a million pieces as I watched the casket being placed in the ground. After the service was over, everyone ran to their cars and pulled off. Rocco and I headed toward his car and hopped inside. We sat there for a moment as the rain pounded down on the window shield.

"I think Dad would be happy about how we put him away," Rocco mumbled.

"Of course, he would. We spent over thirty grand on

his funeral. I'm sure he's satisfied," I assured him.

"Thank you, Ace, for being here, for keeping it a hundred with me, and just being a brother to me."

"I wouldn't have it any other way. You family, nigga. I ain't gonna leave my family. We in this shit together," I told Rocco emotionally.

Rocco and I were all each other had. There was no way we were about to turn our backs on one another. Now that Uncle Dro was gone, we were going to have to stick together. When Rocco pulled up at my house twenty minutes later, it still was raining hard as hell. We both pulled out our umbrellas and ran toward my house. After we had made it safely inside, Rocco headed straight toward the kitchen and began to pour us both some Hennessy. I headed up the stairs and grabbed a bag of weed from my dresser drawer and headed back downstairs to find Rocco sipping on his liquor and staring into space. When he saw me with the weed, he quickly put his cup down and gave me his full attention.

"Bro, I swear, you know exactly what I need right about now."

I took a seat next to him and started sipping on the drink he poured me while he rolled him a fat blunt. I wanted nothing more than to escape the pain that I was feeling inside, but I wasn't in the mood to get high. There was no reason to do all that when the problem was still going to be there when you became sober. As I sipped on my liquor, I couldn't stop thinking about Harmony. She crossed my mind often but today she was on my mind very heavily. The fact that I couldn't forget her name or how she looked let me knew that it was something about her that had caught my eye.

Even though I always said I would never fuck with another nigga girl, Harmony was the one who was the exception to that rule. I wanted to get to know her and it was time that I did just that I mean what did I have to lose? Either she replied, or she didn't. Just because she was rocking a diamond ring didn't mean that she was in love with the nigga or that their relationship was solid enough to even take it further. I pulled my phone from my pocket, went straight to my contacts, and sent Harmony a message. If she didn't respond, then I knew without a doubt that she was happy with the nigga that she was with, but if she did respond, then I was going to take it further and give her whatever she felt like she wasn't getting from her nigga, at least that was what I was telling myself.

I could tell that Harmony wasn't like those other gold digging ass bitches trying to make a come up. She was holding down a job, and I could tell she was very independent. I loved a female that was willing to do shit on her own and not depend on a nigga to give her everything. When I first laid eyes on her, I knew in my soul that Harmony was wifey material. I hoped whoever she was with was treating her right because if he was slacking and I slid in to pick Harmony's broken heart up, it was going to be game over. He wasn't going to get Harmony back.

# CHAPTER 7

# HARMONY

# A WEEK LATER...

Getting my test results back and learning that I was negative of all STD's was what really opened my eyes up to what could have been. I thanked the man above every single day that I opened my eyes that he had protected me even when I had no clue that I needed protection. Kannon had no clue that I was planning on leaving his ass. Enough was enough. There was no way I could continue our relationship when he was fucking around with other bitches and spreading diseases.

I rolled over and noticed that I was in bed alone. I looked over at the clock that was on my nightstand and noticed that it was three in the morning. I had no clue where Kannon was, but I figured he was somewhere he had no business being. Since Torri had spilled all his tea, Kannon had been avoiding me like the plague. Well, let me rephrase that. He and I had been avoiding one another. Hardly any words had been spoken since Torri left that fateful night. Even though he had tried telling me that she was lying, I knew deep in my heart that the bitch was telling me the truth.

I didn't want Kannon touching me period, and for the first time, he and I laid in bed every night, barely saying two words to one another. I was angry that the man I loved would cheat on me and not even wrap his dick up. He really disgusted me. I found myself wanting to throw up every time that I thought back on the many times I had sucked his dick. I had no other choice but to leave his ass. The STD scare was enough to pack my bags and get the fuck out there, but I knew Kannon very well. There was no way I was about to get my ass out of the house alive if he knew I was planning on leaving.

I valued my life, so I made sure that all my tracks were covered. For a whole week straight, I had been hiding money and packing my bags slowly. Every night, when he came home from doing whatever, I made sure to have his meal cooked and made sure to keep my mouth shut and not say no crazy shit to get my ass beat the fuck up. Bria had already told me that I could move in with her, and even though I felt I was going to be intruding, she quickly told my ass that I wasn't. As I lie in bed, tears started to fall from my eyes. I was going to have to leave everything. I hated to leave my house and candy apple read Beamer, but I had no other choice. I wanted my freedom, and I was willing to give up everything to get it. For over a week, I was barely able to sleep. I stayed up most of the night, wondering how I was going to live without the money that I had with Kannon. I had never been a materialistic bitch, but I had gotten used to how Kannon had spoiled me.

I groaned when I stared at the clock yet again. It was about to be six in the morning, I was still up, and Kannon still was out in the streets. It was time for me to stop stressing and try to get some sleep. I closed my eyes as sleep finally found me.

*******

## LATER THAT DAY

I had finally gotten up and was taking a long ass hot shower when my mind began to put two plus two together. Even though I was glad that my test results had come back negative, I still had no proof that Kannon really had herpes. I hadn't found anything that gave me actual proof. I was just going by what another bitch was saying. Even though I believed the hoe, I still needed proof for when I left his nasty ass. After I had hopped out the shower, I decided to do a little snooping around to see what I could find. If he had genital herpes, he was going to be on some type of medicine to keep it at bay. I hurried up and got dressed, pulled my Remy weave in a bun, dabbed a small amount of makeup on my caramel skin, applied some lip-gloss to my juicy lips, and made sure to apply some eyeliner under my eyes so I wouldn't look sleepy. After I was done getting dressed, I admired my slim figure in the mirror before setting out on my task of finding out the truth. I searched his closet from top to bottom but found nothing. I searched his nightstand and even his side of the bathroom where he kept his medicine. I should have known that he wouldn't hide it anywhere where I could find it because I would have known what he had been doing. I hurried downstairs and searched the kitchen where we kept more medicine, but I found nothing there either.

*Where would I hide some medicine that I didn't want anyone to find?* I asked myself.

After thinking for over twenty minutes straight, I decided to check his office, but I still came up with nothing. I was about to give up when something caught my eye in his office. My heart began to pound as I walked toward the bookshelf and moved the picture of him and I kissing. The picture seemed out of place, and that was what threw me off and made me want to see what exactly was behind that picture. I was disappointed when I didn't find anything. I was just about to place the picture back when I noticed a part of the bookshelf looked to have been cut out and placed back together. I pushed the part that looked altered and was shocked to see two small bottles of Valtrex. At first, I didn't know what the fuck the drug was until I pulled out my iPhone and asked Siri if she knew what it was. I waited as she searched and gave me the best possible answer. When I found out that Valtrex was to prevent a severe outbreak of herpes, I literally almost fell out. Tears welled in my eyes as I read his name and the month he had the bottle filled.

Even though I knew he probably had this shit, I still was in shock that I was right. I was beyond angry and disgusted that that nigga could have passed me that shit. The fact that he knew was what really pissed me off. I wiped the last bit of my tears and finally made up my mind that I had all the proof I needed to get the hell away from him. I wanted to leave him that very night if I could. I heard the front door open, and I quickly placed the bottle back in its hiding spot, put everything back in place, and got the fuck out of this office before he saw me there. I was just about to head into the living room when I spotted Kannon dressed in all black from his head to his feet.

"Where you going?" he asked with irritation in his voice.

I decided to choose my words carefully, but I could tell that he was in a bad mood just by how he was looking at me all sideways.

"I'm about to head over to Bria's house for a quick minute."

Kannon walked toward me, and my whole body began to shake.

*Please, don't touch me,* I kept begging in my head.

"Don't be gone all day. You and I need to talk when you get back home. I'm tired of us giving one another this silent treatment."

I didn't trust myself to speak. Instead, I grabbed the keys to my Beamer and got the fuck out of there.

I did almost seventy as I sped through the city to Bria's house. When I pulled up at her spot, I hopped out and banged on her door.

"Bitch, why the fuck are you banging on my door like you the motherfucking police?" Bria asked.

I didn't respond. I just stormed into her house and headed straight to her kitchen and quickly poured me a small glass of Tequila. I took close to four shots to the head before I looked over at Bria, who was staring at me with wide eyes.

"Damn, bitch, what's going on with you?"

I was silent, and Bria dipped out the kitchen and came back with a small bag of weed. I followed her into the living room and watched as she rolled a blunt and lit that bitch on fire. Bria took a puff before passing it to me.

"Bria, I can't smoke that shit. I be having pop up drug tests at the daycare I work at."

"Fuck that damn job, Harmony. Now, smoke this damn blunt. It will calm your little ass down."

I looked at Bria and noticed she was serious as hell. I groaned, took the blunt, and took three puffs before I began coughing.

"Take those puffs slowly, Harmony. Damn, this some good shit here."

Tears stung my eyes, and I wiped them away.

"Now, tell me what's going on with you?" Bria asked patiently.

"The rumors are true. Kannon got that shit. My test results came back negative earlier this week, but I couldn't wrap my mind around whether he had herpes or not."

I became silent as I took a small pull from the blunt.

"I went snooping around, and boom, I find his medicine bottle in his office hid inside the bookshelf." Bria shook her head.

"Now that you got the proof, what are you going to do now?"

"Bria, I'm close to throwing up right about now. Just knowing he knew he had this shit and was trying to spread this shit to me is what got me pissed the fuck off. Now that I got proof, I'm dipping out on his ass. Right now, he home, but as soon as he dip out again, I'm leaving also. Deep down in my heart, I knew Torri's hoe ass was telling me the truth, so I already been packing and shit. I also got a little saved up that he been throwing my way."

Bria embraced me in a hug and pointed me to the long hallway where my room would be at.

I stood up from the couch and followed Bria toward the back where she was pointing at. She slowly turned the knob and I stood there with my mouth wide open as I took the whole room in.

"This going to be your room, sis. Tay and my room upstairs, so nobody will be in the others way. You can stay as long as you want."

The room was big as hell, with a king-sized bed, a sixty-five-inch flat screen TV, a bathroom to myself, and it was neatly decorated in my favorite color, purple. I turned around with tears in my eyes.

"Thanks, Bria. I'm so lucky to have you in my life."

She smiled down at me before placing a small kiss on my cheek.

"I'm always going to be here for you, sis."

Bria and I smoked for most of the day. I was high as hell, so I knew there was no way I was going to be able to get my ass home anytime soon. When I heard Travis Scott blasting from my phone, I jumped up, and my heart felt as if it was about to beat out my chest. I pulled the phone from my pocket, expecting to see Kannon's name displayed on the front of my screen, but instead, it was a text message from a number that I didn't recognize. When I opened the text and saw that it was from Ace, my heart skipped, a beat and I found it hard to even breathe. Butterflies tickled my stomach because I wasn't expecting to hear from Ace. It had been close to three weeks since he and I had met, but there he was, texting my phone, apologizing for not hitting me up sooner. I began to smile hard as hell, and I guess Bria noticed. She scooted closer to me and asked who I was texting. I moved the phone from her view and smirked.

"Ain't you being nosy?" I joked.

"Shid, I want to know who got your ass lighting up like you a damn Christmas tree over there. I know damn well it ain't Kannon's bitch ass."

"Nah, it ain't Kannon. Remember that nigga I was telling you about a few weeks ago? His name is Ace, and I met him at the daycare. Well, he finally texted me. To be honest, I didn't think I was going to hear from his ass."

"Harmony, that's what's up. I'm so glad that you ain't stressing over the Kannon shit anymore.

"I'm just glad that I'm going to be officially single soon."

"You should have been single, but that's a whole new story right there."

I bit down on my bottom lip and began to let my mind wonder. I was drunk and high, so I wasn't thinking logically. I had to make sure I got out of my relationship with Kannon alive and in one piece before I tried fucking around with Ace. For all I knew, Ace probably already had a bitch, but I didn't give two fucks if he did have a bitch already. None of those other bitches cared about me being with Kannon. They were still trying to ride his dick, even when they knew he had someone, so why should I give a fuck about fucking with the next bitch's nigga?

Bria and I chilled for a little while longer, and I sat there and texted Ace the whole time. Just before I was about to turn on Bria's Netflix, I received a phone call from Kannon. Instead of answering the bitch, I sent Kannon's ass to voicemail, which I knew would piss him off. It was eleven at night, and there was no way I was ready to head home just yet.

"You know that nigga gonna keep blowing up your phone until you pick up."

I rolled my eyes and flipped the TV to the ID channel when I couldn't find anything to watch on Netflix. Bria fired up another blunt, and we talked about all the shit I would be doing when I got away from Kannon. My heart began to race when my phone began to ring yet again. When Ace's named popped up on the screen, I felt my stomach do summersaults. I took a few deep breaths before I answered. When his voice filled my ears, my heart began to thump hard as hell.

"Hey," I managed to choke out into the phone.

"Hey, Harmony. What you up to? Did I wake you?"

"I'm chilling at my homegirl house, and no, you ain't wake me."

"Good, I just wanted to hear your voice for a quick minute. I enjoyed texting you."

I blushed, and Bria smacked my thigh.

"I didn't think you were going to message me," I said honestly.

"I'm sorry about that. I've been going through so much that I didn't want to throw any bad vibes your way. I just buried my uncle, so I've been going through a lot. He was like a father to me."

I leaned up from the couch and made sure that I paid close attention to what Ace was saying.

"When I first met you, I instantly felt something for you. I know you got a nigga, and I ain't trying to cause no problems. I just want to get to know you better."

"I won't be having a man for long. A lot of shit been going on with my life as well since we met, so I understand why you ain't reach out to me earlier. It probably was for the best because I was in a dark place with the nigga I'm with."

"Harmony, you a queen. If he ain't treating you like what you are, then you need to dip out on that nigga. I'm not trying to get all in your business, but if you need me, you got my number."

When Ace said that shit, I swear, I felt it in my damn soul. We talked for over two hours before my phone went dead. I quickly put that bitch on the charger and was met by Bria who was staring daggers at me.

"Damn, you just pulled your ass a real ass nigga. I like his ass already."

I laughed at her ass because she had actually laid there and listened to my whole damn conversation.

"Sis, I'm proud of you. So glad you about to dip out on Kannon's dirty dick ass."

I groaned and rubbed my face because it was one in the morning, and I wasn't home. I already knew when I made it there that Kannon was going to be all in my face. I grabbed my keys and kissed Bria on the cheek. She held me tightly in her arms before asking me if I was sure I wanted to leave.

"I might as well take my ass home and face him now. I can't keep on avoiding him."

The expression on Bria's face told me otherwise. When she told me to wait where I was at until she came back, I knew instantly that she was up to something. My eyes grew wide when she brought me back her purple Glock and told me to take it with me.

"Bria, I'm not going to need that."

"Harmony, take it just in case. I already know you know how to aim and shoot. Don't hesitate to put a bullet in him if you need to," Bria told me seriously.

I held the gun in my hand before I handed it back to her.

"Thanks, boo, but I will be good."

Bria, rolled her eyes and placed her gun on the couch and walked me to the door. I turned around and embraced Bria in a hug before I noticed her eyes were bloodshot red. She was high as hell and was probably about to go in her room and knock the hell out.

I pulled up at my house twenty minutes later. The porch light was on, but everything else in the house was pitch dark. I was still a little high, but I was sobering up rather quickly as I ran up the steps to the front door. I had just stepped into the house when Kannon flipped on the lamp. He was sitting in the living room in the chair by the window. He was dressed in a pair of black Nike basketball shorts, a red shirt, black Nike socks, and a pair of red and black Nike sandals. I could tell by how he was looking at me that he was pissed the fuck off.

"I've been calling your phone all damn night and got no answer. Matter fact, your ass sent me to voicemail a few times."

I looked at him like he was crazy because I had no clue how long he had been sitting in the damn dark waiting for me to come home.

"My phone went dead, and I told you I was going to be with Bria."

Kannon stood up and walked over to me.

"When I call your ass, I expect for you to pick up the fucking phone. I don't give a fuck what your ass doing."

I didn't know if it was the liquor or if it was just me fed up with his bullshit. There was no way I was about to stand there and let that nigga walk all over me any longer. For the first time, I was ready to stand up for myself and look that nigga dead in the eye. The liquor had me feeling good, so I didn't think twice before I told him what I knew.

"Nigga, don't step to me like you own me because you don't. I'm a grown ass woman. Like I said, I was with Bria, and my phone went dead."

Kannon balled his fists up, and I looked him dead in the eye,

"So, now you mad, huh? I think you ain't got shit to be mad about. I'm the one who should be mad. Nigga, you ain't never been faithful or loyal, and I still stuck by your side, but this shit you and I have right here is coming to an end. I know your secret, the one you got hid in your office inside the bookshelf. I know you got that shit, and your nasty dick ass didn't even tell me. I thank God every day he protected me," I spat at Kannon.

I was being brave as hell and had said everything that I had wanted to say. I noticed the anger in his eyes, but he said nothing. He just stared at me. If looks could have killed, I would have been dead.

"I'm leaving you, Kannon… for good this time."

*Smack!*

The slap stung my cheek, and I held it with my hand.

"Bitch, you ain't going nowhere. You belong to me. The only way you leaving me is if your ass is six feet deep."

I tried backing away from him, but he snatched my ass up, wrapped his hands around my neck, and he wouldn't let go. I closed my eyes tightly as I felt myself drifting away to another place.

"If you think for one minute that I'm about to let you leave, then you are sadly mistaken. If you even try leaving me, I promise you I will find you and make you wish you never left," he whispered vehemently in my ear.

I felt chills up my spine and arm as his words began to run deep in my soul. When he let me go, I fell to the floor, gasping for air. I crawled on my hands and knees toward my purse, but when his foot hit my back, I cried out in pain. Every time he hit me, I begged him to stop, but my cries went unheard. Instead of him walking away and leaving me alone, he grabbed me by my hair and yanked me up off the ground before punching me in the mouth.

"Next time, you pick up the fucking phone," he replied angrily before grabbing his keys and dipping out the house.

I grabbed my Gucci bag and slowly made my way upstairs. Tears fell down my face as I headed toward the bathroom. I stared at myself in the mirror and noticed my lip was busted, and I was rocking a black eye. I removed my clothes and noticed bruises covering my neck, my back, my chest, and stomach. I wiped the blood that was leaking from my lip and ran some water in the bathtub. I had no clue when Kannon was going to be back, but I prayed he stayed away long enough for me to be gone before he came back home.

I soaked in the tub for over forty-five minutes before I stepped out and dried my bruised body. I quickly got dressed and pulled my hair into a ponytail. I slid on my black Air Forces and grabbed the bags that I had secretly been packing all week long. I grabbed my phone to dial Bria's number to let her know that I was leaving Kannon, but her phone sent me straight to voicemail. I cursed under my breath. That only meant one thing the bitch was wasted, and her phone was dead. It was time that I accepted the fact that I wasn't going to hear from her ass until sometime later that morning. I wanted to get out while I could. I was ready to be free before Kannon came back home and saw all my shit packed up. I didn't want that nigga to nut up and try to kill me.

I would have called an Uber, but I wasn't in the mood to go to the play store to download the app and verify all my damn information to even pay for a ride. I hated to get Ace involved, but I had no other choice. I was desperate at the moment. My heart thumped as I waited for Ace to pick up the phone. Damn, what the fuck was I doing? I barely knew the nigga and had only talked with him for only two hours that was not enough time to ask that nigga for a favor.

I closed my eyes and was relieved when I heard his deep voice fill my ears.

"Ace, I'm sorry to bother you, but I couldn't call anyone else for help."

"What's wrong, Harmony?" Ace asked with alarm in his voice.

My hands began to shake as I tried holding back the tears from falling down my face.

"Can you please come pick me up? I will explain everything when you get here."

"Give me your address, and I will be right over."

I rattled off my address and hung up the phone. I wanted to apply a little makeup to hide some of the bruises, but I decided against the shit. I wasn't really in the mood to dig through my suitcase to find any makeup at the moment. I hurried and grabbed my two suitcases, cut off all the lights upstairs, and headed downstairs so I could hear Ace when he pulled up. I sat at the coffee table, pulled out a small sheet of paper and a pen, and started to write Kannon a small note, letting him know that I was gone.

*If you are reading this, then I'm far away from you. Do not try to find me because I don't want to be found. Just leave me alone, and let me live my life without you in it. You have done nothing for me but hurt me, lie to me, and cheat on me, but you claim you love me. Well, if this is love, then I don't want it. Here is your ring. The wedding is off. We are done.*

144

Twenty minutes later, I heard a car pull up in my driveway, and a couple seconds later I heard the horn blowing outside. I took a peek outside and noticed Ace was stepping out the car looking sexy as hell. I grabbed my two suitcases and looked back at the house one last time before saying goodbye. I dropped my keys on the table by the front door and made sure to leave Kannon's small note right beside it. When he finally brought his ass home, he was going to see a dark house and no Harmony.

As soon as my feet hit the ground, I felt free. Ace grabbed the suitcases from my hand and placed them in the back of his small trunk before we both hopped in the car. I tried covering my face, but it was way too late. Ace spotted my busted lip and black eye as soon as the light in the car hit my caramel skin.

"What the fuck happened to your face?" Ace asked angrily.

I was silent for a moment, and I guess Ace decided to figure it out on his own.

"I know damn well this nigga ain't put his hand on you. Where that nigga at? Is he still in the house?"

When I saw Ace pull out his gun my eyes grew big, and I instantly grabbed him by the arm.

"He ain't in there, Ace, and even if he was, I wasn't about to let you go in there and kill him. Let's just go," I pleaded with him.

I could tell how Ace was looking that he was pissed the fuck off. He gripped the steering wheel tightly as he pulled into traffic. I was quiet and made sure to not say nothing that would cause Ace to flip out again.

"How long has this nigga been hitting you?"

I licked my lips and pulled my weave away from my face before I answered his question.

"Since we been together."

"How long, Harmony?"

"Six years," I mumbled.

Ace sighed with frustration, and I watched him out the corner of my eye as he rubbed his hands through his short-trimmed haircut.

"You way to damn beautiful to be letting a nigga put his hands on you. If I could, I would fuck that nigga up because I was raised to never hit a damn female. He wrong for that shit. I bet he won't hit no nigga but quick to hit a female."

I looked out the window as he and I weaved in and out of traffic.

"Do you want me to take you somewhere?" Ace asked more gently.

"I was supposed to go to my homegirl Bria's spot, but she done went to sleep, and her phone dead."

Ace nodded his head as pulled into Burger King and turned back around into traffic.

"You can stay at my spot tonight until you figure out what you want to do in the morning.

I wanted to object, but I had no reason to. I was just grateful that I had Ace in my life at the moment. I had no clue how long he was planning on staying, but how he had shown up and saved the day had me in my feelings.

"Is this your spot?" I asked Ace curiously as he pulled up to his house a few moments later.

"Yes, this all mines."

Soon as I stepped inside, I was amazed at just how big it was.

"This is so nice," I whispered.

"Thanks," Ace said before carrying my bags down the hallway.

I quickly followed him down the hallway as my heart began to beat erratically.

*Which room is he taking me to?* I wondered.

I began to panic because I knew nothing about the nigga. He was nice as hell to take me in, but maybe he had a motive. Maybe he wanted some ass in return. Was I going to give it to him so early in the game? So many thoughts were running through my brain, and I had no answers to any of them.

When we made our way toward the last door at the end of the hall, I was shocked to see that I had my own room along with my own bathroom. The room was decorated in hot pink and cream with a king-sized bed, a big black dresser, a fifty-inch TV with a little girl's toy box, and a big walk-in closet.

"I hope you don't mind, but this is Jasmine's room when she comes over and visits."

"It's perfect," I mumbled.

"If you need anything, just let me know. All the bath cloths and towels are in the bathroom already. My room is beside yours if you may need me for whatever reason."

He stared at me, licked his lips, and my knees grew weak. My body felt as if I was on fire, but I blamed it on the lack of dick that I had been getting from Kannon. Just thinking of Kannon put me in a foul mood.

When Ace placed his hand on my bruised cheek, I shivered.

"You so beautiful. I want you to know that I'm here if you need me."

"Thank you."

I couldn't take my eyes off of Ace as he stared at me with so much intensity in his eyes. I was sort of disappointed when he moved away from me, placed my bags on my bed, and left the room. After I heard his door shut behind him, I took a seat on the bed, pulled out my phone, and shot Bria a message to let her know that I had left Kannon, and I was safe with Ace for the night. I unzipped my smallest suitcase and began to count some of the money that I had taken from Kannon when he wasn't looking. What he didn't know wouldn't hurt him. I closed the suitcase and placed it in the closet along with the suitcase with my clothes. I had half a million dollars, and that alone was enough for me to start over. But deep in my heart, I knew Kannon wasn't going to let me go so easily.

# CHAPTER 8

## ROCCO

Since my dad had passed, I was still trying to get my life back on track. I barely was able to get up in the mornings or even hustle on the block. I had always been about my cash, so I knew my dad being gone was what had set me back. If it wasn't for London coming over on the regular and checking up on a nigga, there was no telling where I would be.

London and I had been through a lot of shit, but when a nigga's dad died, London had been here for me every step of the way. She came over every damn day and cooked me a hot meal, cleaned up my house for me, and kept me company. I appreciated everything she had done because if I had been left alone for even a second, I believe I would have gone straight crazy.

At one point in time, London was the main source of my stress, but lately, she was stepping up to the plate and doing better with herself. Not once had Lil' Quan hit me up about something that he had seen London doing. She had just landed a part-time job at Verizon and was making her own money and wasn't trying to gold dig. I had nothing but respect and love for my baby mama. Hearing my phone blast Gucci Mane woke me from my daze. I picked up my phone when I noticed Ace calling me.

"Bro, you good?" Ace asked.

"Yeah, everything straight over this way. I'm still hurting, but I'm trying to get it together."

"Me too, bro. I miss Uncle Dro. Damn, I still can't believe he gone," Ace cried into the phone.

Even though my dad was no longer on this earth, Ace and I had enough money to take care of ourselves, and we had that street mentality to survive this cold world. When Ace asked what my plans were from there on out, I became quiet for a moment. The only plans I had was to expand and make more money, but I had no clue if my day one nigga was going to be down.

"Ace, I'm going to keep it real with you, bro. I want to do bigger and better things. I want to expand and shit, but I want to make sure that you gonna be down."

"Rocco, you know I'm down to get more paper, but I think its best if we leave the street shit alone and go legit.

I know you don't want to do that shit, but Uncle Dro's last wish was for us to let that street shit go."

I didn't speak at first because my brain was racing. I wasn't ready to give up the streets I loved the power and the bitches that it brought to me.

"Ace, I hear what you saying, but I ain't ready to go legit. I mean, it ain't no money in giving up the street life. I'm my own man. I've been in the streets all my damn life. No way I'm leaving to get some clean money."

I could hear the frustration in Ace's voice, but there was nothing that Ace could do and say to make me change my damn mind. Just because he wanted to do the right thing didn't mean I was about to follow his lead.

"Rocco, you always been stubborn, but this ain't the time. With the money I got from my dad and the money Uncle Dro left, I've decided to open up a night club. Do you know how much money I'm going to bring in?" Ace asked seriously.

"It sounds good, bro, I'm down to support, but that's not what I want to do for myself."

Ace was silent and didn't speak. I pulled the phone

from my ear to make sure he was still on the line.

"Rocco, do what you got to do, bro, but be careful. I'm done with the streets."

"Cool, Ace. I see you and I want two different things, but I ain't mad at ya."

"Whatever you do, Rocco, don't trust Young G. I know you want to expand, but trusting his ass ain't wise. Something about that nigga ain't right. It has never been. I always felt like that nigga was a snitch and a hating ass nigga. I know you don't believe he is, but just think hard. How did Lil' Eddy get caught last year with that dope in his car? Young G and him was tight as hell. Even though we didn't fuck with Lil' Eddy growing up, I know he was Young G's right-hand nigga, so when he got busted with all that dope and Young G was nowhere to be found, I felt he had something to do with the shit. That nigga can't be trusted Rocco."

I listened to Ace because I already knew he wanted me to know what I was getting myself into, but deep down inside, I was itching to get more cash and not really bothered by what Ace was telling me about Young G.

There was no way that Young G had anything to do with Lil' Eddy getting caught up and busted with a car full of dope. Lil' Eddy had fucked around and had probably told his bitch his business, and she had set his ass up.

Ace and I talked for a little while longer before he told me he was going to pull up at my crib later on. After getting off the phone, I headed toward the bathroom so I could freshen up for later that day. After I had gotten dressed and had pulled my dreads back in a ponytail, I grabbed my keys and headed toward London's spot so I could see my baby Jasmine. When I pulled up at my baby mama's house, I wasn't expecting to see another car parked in her driveway. I didn't know who she had over, but I was soon about to find out. I had a key to her house, so I pulled that bitch out my pocket, walked right in the house, and found London ass laying down on the couch while her younger cousin, Lil' Don was sitting in a chair rolling him a blunt while watching a movie on Netflix. London hopped up when she saw me and asked what I was doing there.

"Damn, I pay bills in this bitch. I can come up here anytime I damn want to."

I could tell how London was eyeing me up that she was about to get smart with a nigga.

"I came to see my baby. Where she at?"

"She upstairs sleeping."

Lil' Don dapped me up before he lit his blunt. He took a long puff before blowing the smoke out his nose. London gave her cousin the look to get the fuck up and leave, but Lil' Don didn't budge.

London rolled her eyes and grabbed me by the hand before leading me upstairs to her bedroom. I took a seat on the bed beside her and held her in my arms. I had never just held London like I was doing at that very moment. I'd never been the type of nigga to give a fuck about any bitch, but after London had switched up and started acting like a woman and not a hoe, how I treated her slowly began to change. When I first pulled up, I had no clue who London had in this bitch. If it would have been a nigga she was fucking with, I would have smacked the bitch and asked questions later. I closed my eyes as she rubbed her hands through my dreads.

****

I don't know how long I slept, but when I woke up, I was alone. I stretched, pulled out my phone, and noticed it was nine at night. I slid out of London's bed and followed the voices to the kitchen where I found London's fine ass cooking some white rice with smothered pork chops and Jiffy cornbread. My stomach began to growl as I watched her fix Jasmine a small plate.

"Daddy!" Jasmine yelled out.

I walked over to my baby and placed a kiss on her cheek before tickling her gently. Jasmine giggled and laughed loudly. Seeing Jasmine smiling and laughing made me feel good as hell. I knew I wasn't perfect, but to see my daughter's eyes glow as soon as I walked in the room, that told me that I was doing something right. I walked toward London and hugged her from the back before placing a kiss on her cheek.

"This food smells good," I whispered in her ear.

"Thanks, babe." She giggled.

She handed me my plate that she had just fixed, and I quickly took a seat at the table. I was just about to dig in to eat when she popped my hand.

"Baby, we have to say grace."

I looked at London in disbelief but nodded my head and took her hand as we said our grace.

I had been so hurt about my dad passing that I had not once prayed since he closed his eyes. I didn't hate God, but I hated the fact that he took my dad away from me. As I ate my food, I noticed that London was barely eating.

"Boo, what's wrong? Why ain't you eating?"

London didn't look me in the eye directly, so I knew something was going on with her. The fact that I didn't know what the fuck was wrong with her was fucking with me hard as hell. London licked her lips before staring me in the eye.

"Rocco, I just want you to know that I love you. I know I've done a lot of fucked up shit in the past, but now, it's time to change. I want us to grow closer, raise Jasmine, and respect each other. Even if you not ready to be in a relationship right about now, that's cool. I understand that. No pressure… no stressing over it. Regardless, I'm always going to be in your corner, and you will always be the nigga who I rock with."

Damn, London was speaking some real shit, even my heart felt that shit. I didn't hesitate to pull her out of her chair and embrace her in a tight hug. I pulled away from her briefly as I caressed her cheek.

"London, I love you. Thanks for being here helping me through hard time that I'm facing."

London didn't speak. She just kissed me gently on my lips. My dick started to rise, but I quickly had to get myself in check because when I turned around, I noticed Jasmine staring at me with her big beautiful eyes. I made sure to help London clean the kitchen back up and played with Jasmine until she fell to sleep. I held Jasmine in my arms tightly as I carried her to her bed and tucked her in. When my phone went off, I quickly pulled it out of my pocket to see who was texting me. When I noticed it was one of my hoes that I used to fuck with, I quickly ignored the shit. Instead of leaving for the night like I would have done in the past, I decided to stay a little while longer and spend some time with London. It was time that I also stepped up to the plate and gave London exactly what she was begging for. Before I headed back to check on London, I quickly blocked the hoe who had just texted me.

"Is she sleep already?" London asked just before she stepped out the bathroom with a towel wrapped around her body.

"Yes, she out and going to sleep until the next morning."

"Good," London said as she walked over to where I was sitting on the bed and placed her lips on mines.

We were just about to deepen the kiss when my phone began to ring. I picked up because it was Ace calling.

"What up, bro?"

"Nun much. Just about to come through. You home?" Ace asked.

"Nah, I ain't home. I ain't gonna be back until the morning. I'm with London."

Just when I thought Ace was going to say some slick shit, he said something that had my mind blown.

"Be safe, Rocco. I know you love shorty, but make sure you know what you doing. Life too short to be living it with regrets and makin' decisions that you will have to pay for until your black ass leave this earth."

Whether Ace knew it or not, I was safe because I finally knew what I wanted out of my life, and that was my family.

I ended the call, and that's when London slid off the bed and tried to walk off. There was no way I was about to let her get in her feelings about my conversation with Ace. London and Ace had never really gotten along like that, because when Ace first met London, she was on that bullshit. He quickly put her in that category of bitches who wasn't about shit.

"Baby, what's wrong?"

"Nothing," she mumbled as she headed into the bathroom.

Of course, me being me, I followed behind her. I watched but didn't speak as she turned on the shower. She looked back at me with attitude and asked if I could leave while she showered in peace.

I raised an eyebrow at her before I grabbed her by the arm.

"I'm not going anywhere until you get rid of the

attitude. I already know you probably pissed about what you heard Ace say over the phone, but get out your feelings, baby. Ace still believes you the messy bitch who wanted to ruin my life. He just wants me to be careful, that's all."

My heart broke when I noticed tears forming in her eyes.

"I'm so tired of people judging me for what I used to do and what I used to be. People change, Rocco. I've changed."

"Shhhhh, baby, don't cry," I said gently as I wrapped her small body into my arms. I held her as she cried.

"Baby, try to calm down. I know you have changed, and I will make sure to explain to Ace exactly what is going on because he doesn't know. We have a lot of shit going on, so things just been crazy with Ace and I, but just know I will get him straight about you."

London pulled away from me and nodded her head.

"Yeah, you do that," she mumbled.

I pulled her hair away from her face and placed a kiss on her forehead before kissing her juicy lips. London softly moaned, and I took that as the sign that I could go farther. I pulled her white top over her head just before I pulled her black booty shorts from her firm ass. London stepped out her black thong before unsnapping her bra. She smirked at me before she stepped her fine ass into the tub.

I hurried and undressed so I could join her in the shower. As the hot water pounded down on our bodies, our lips found one another yet again. I pushed London gently up against the shower wall and turned her around so she wasn't facing the water that was pounding down on the both of us. I pushed open her legs and moved her long weave to the side just before I slid my hard dick into her tight pussy.

"Shiiittt," I managed to moan out as I began to slide in and out of her sweet juicy pussy.

London began to whine as I gripped her hair in my hand and began to pound her pussy with force.

"Fuck me harder," London managed to croak out.

London had always been the type of bitch that I could fuck as hard as I wanted. She loved the rough sex, and being me who I was, I loved dicking a bitch down who wasn't afraid to take my big dick.

I bit down on her neck as I pushed in and out of her a few more times before I turned around her around to face me. I stared deeply into her eyes as I picked her up, and she wrapped her legs around my waist.

"I love you," she whispered just before I slid back into her.

Her screams filled the bathroom as I fucked her until she was nutting all over my dick. I slammed into her a few more times before I busted all my nut inside of her. After I was done fucking her brains out, I stepped away from her for only a brief moment as I began to wash her body clean. She continued to keep her hands placed on the shower tile as I washed every inch of her. After I was done washing her, I moved aside to let her rinse the soap suds from her body. I waited until she was out of the shower before I stepped under the hot water and closed my eyes. As the water pounded down on my face, I decided it was time to accept the changes that fate had given me. My father was no longer here on this Earth, and even though I found myself crying myself to sleep every fucking night, I knew deep down in my heart that my father was in a better place. The only thing that kept me from getting back into that dark place was knowing that I had London, my beautiful daughter, and I was in a position to gain more than I had ever had.

******

### <u>3 DAYS LATER</u>

I had just pulled up at the abandoned building and was waiting for Ace to pull up next to me. Ace had been searching all week long for a building that met the qualifications to be turned into a nightclub. Clubs came in all sizes, but Ace wanted the club to big enough for people all over the city to come through and have a good time. When he told me he had found a big enough building and sent me to check it out, I didn't hesitate to show my nigga some support.

The whole time that I was waiting for this nigga to come, I surfed the internet for a while until an engagement ring ad caught my attention. Immediately, I began to think about London, and I instantly began to get scared as hell. I never thought about marrying any bitch. I swear I thought my heart had softened since my dad was no longer here. I learned from my dad dying that you never knew when it was going to be your time to die. We all had to die, so as long as I had breath in my body, I was going to get my money and live like it was my last day.

Just when I felt myself slipping back into a depressive state, I quickly snapped out of it when I noticed that my nigga Young G was calling me. Young G and I hadn't really talked since I went with him to Marietta, Georgia, to meet up with another connect. I wanted more money than I was making, and the fact that I was trying to take on a family was what motivated me even more to get in with those niggas from Marietta. If Ace wasn't going to go along for the ride, then I guess I was going to have to go at it alone. Ace wanted out of the game, and I was just about to get started. There was no way I was ready to leave the streets.

"Rocco, my niggas say they down to do business if you

ready to make a move."

I rubbed my chin as I thought carefully about my response.

"Young G, you know I'm always down to make some money, so you already know my answer is going to be hell yeah."

"Cool, I will let them know, and they will hit your ass up."

"You and Ace still rocking as a team?"

"Nah, I think Ace want out the game."

"Too bad," Young G replied.

I could tell in Young G's voice that he didn't give two fucks if Ace was down or not. Young G and I talked for a little while longer before I spotted Ace's Aston Martin pull up next to me.

"I'ma hit you later, Young G."

"Okay cool."

I stepped out of my Porsche and dapped Ace up.

"I think this will be the perfect building for this club," Ace announced.

We took a look around, and I agreed with Ace on his

decision.

I watched as Ace pulled out his phone and called the number on the front of the sign that was posted outside. After talking to the woman for over thirty minutes and getting all the information about the building, Ace finally made plans to purchase the building. After he ended the call, he asked me what my plans were for the club. I sighed because Ace was still trying to persuade me to leave the street life alone. It was time that I was straight up real with Ace and let him know that I made the decision to build my empire.

"Ace, you and I are on two different paths. You want out the business, and I'm aiming to build me an empire from the ground up. This club you buying, that's your dream."

"Rocco, you like a bro to me, but you know I wouldn't tell you nothing wrong. Before Uncle Dro died, he wanted us both out the game. I promised him I was going to get out and you would too."

I shook my head at Ace and eyed him up all funny.

"I ain't getting out right now. Young G about to hook

me up with the deal, and I'mma take that motherfucka."

I could tell what I said hurt Ace, but I didn't care. Ace was going to have to learn that I was grown, and he couldn't keep telling me what I needed to be doing. I was going to live like I wanted. Ace was just about to say something, but his phone began to ring. When he answered the phone, his face lit up. I couldn't help but listen in on his conversation as he and I stood posted up on his car. Whoever he was talking to had him all in his feelings. Never in my life had I heard that nigga ever call anybody baby, and he was spitting that shit out like it was natural. When Ace ended the call, I eyed that nigga like he was an alien. I mean, who in the hell was the nigga that was standing in front of me. Nah, he wasn't acting like Ace because he was the type of nigga who never let a bitch get close to him.

"What I need to know is who is the female that got your ass acting all soft and shit?"

Ace ignored my question and looked me in the eye.

"Nigga, get off me. Don't let me get on you and London. I just hope your ass ain't letting your guard down with her just yet."

I cleared my throat and stared at him.

"London ain't how she used to be. She part of the reason why I'm not locked away in a hospital some damn where. That bitch came through for a nigga, on the real. She made sure I was straight every damn day. She been standing by me the whole time."

"Damn. I didn't even know that London was even coming around. In that case bro, I hope everything works out for you. I just don't want to see you get hurt."

"I'm good bro, but don't think I ain't catch on with what you just did."

"What I just do?" Ace asked with a smirk on his face.

I chuckled because Ace was doing everything in his power to keep me from knowing who the girl was.

"Who is she, Ace? I'm curious."

"Harmony, Jasmine's teacher."

I laughed hard as hell.

"I can't believe your ass was serious about actually trying to get with her."

"Hell yeah, I'm crazy about her ass. It's like when our

eyes connected, I was drawn to her. Right now, she's at my spot."

"Hold the fuck up, nigga. You already smashed?"

"Hell nah. She ain't like that. I wouldn't dare try her up like that unless she wants this dick, but I don't think shorty ready for this wood. I will fuck her whole life up. She and I are taking things slowly at the moment."

"How the fuck y'all taking things slowly when you got her in your crib by herself, nigga? You must really trust her."

"Yeah, shorty different, and she going through some hard times. Her nigga and her done broke up, and she ain't got nowhere to go right about now."

"Okay. Look at ya trying to be Captain Save a Hoe."

"When I went to pick her ass up, she was rocking bruises with a black eye and shit. I swear, I wanted to murk that nigga."

"Oh, hell nah. Harmony got her an abusive ass nigga."

"She ain't with that nigga no mo'. As long as she with me, that nigga better not step to her because I don't mind putting his ass to sleep."

"I don't blame your ass. We don't lay hands on bitches, but I will smack a bitch if needed but never to make bruises. I just want to smack some sense into the bitch."

Ace and I joked around before he told me he had to dip out and take Harmony to work. I was just about to hop in my whip and dip out when Ace stopped me.

"Bro, I ain't trying to lecture you about your lifestyle and what you want to do, but do me a favor. Watch your back with Young G. I don't trust that nigga. When it comes to the streets, I trust no nigga."

I didn't say nothing back to Ace; instead, I nodded my head to let him know that I heard him. I waited until he had gotten back in his car and pulled off before I hopped in my car and dipped out. The whole ride to London's crib, I began to wonder if fucking around with Young G would be wise, but I quickly pushed the negativity from my mind when I pulled up at London's spot. Time I stepped into the house, I could smell London's Chanel perfume. The sweet scent had a nigga's dick hard as hell and had me ready to suck on London's sweet pussy. When I stepped into London's bedroom, I noticed her in front of the mirror getting ready for work. She was fully dressed and was applying makeup to her chocolate colored face. I walked over to her and smacked her ass before sucking on her earlobe.

She softly moaned before I snatched her makeup out her hand, placed it on the table, picked her sexy ass up, and pushed her up against the wall. Our lips met one another as our tongues wrestled with each other. Most bitches would have pulled away from me and complained that they didn't have time for no quickie, but London was different. She was a freak, and I loved that shit. I put her back down on the ground, and we quickly undid our clothes before making our way to the bed.

I pushed baby girl on her back, slid between her legs, and licked on her clit as I slid my finger in and out her tight pussy. London was moaning and chanting my name loud as hell, but I never once stopped pleasing her until she began to cream on my tongue. I pulled away from her quickly as I stared down at her beautiful body. I rubbed my dick with my spare hand as I played in her pussy with my finger. Seeing her facial expressions while she was being pleased really turned me on. I slid my hard dick into her, wrapped my hands gently around her neck, and we stared deeply into each other's eyes.

She wrapped her legs around my waist as I fucked her with no mercy. Sweat dripped from our bodies as I thrust in and out of her juicy pussy. I slid out of her and put her legs behind her head as I gave her some fast, deep strokes. Just hearing her scream my name had a nigga ready to bust all up in her.

"Fuck me!" London screamed loudly.

A few moments later, I pulled out of her, and that's when I noticed she had milked my whole dick with her white cream.

"This dick good?" I asked her as I slid into her from the side.

"Yes, baby." She whimpered as I slammed into her and played with her erect nipples.

I sucked on her neck as I penetrated London's tight walls. I slowed up my strokes as I tried to savor her pussy. I gripped her titties tightly as I slammed into her a few more times before I caught my nut. I was tired and sweaty but very much satisfied. After we were done, London and I quickly headed into the bathroom to clean ourselves up before putting back on our clothes. When we were all clean, London kissed me on my cheek before grabbing her bag and car keys.

"Are you going to be here when I get off?"

"Nah, I'm going back to my crib."

"Jasmine and I going to hang there until you get off."

"Sounds good. Give Jasmine a kiss for me when you pick her up from daycare."

"Of course, I will," I told London.

I waited until she had dipped out before I headed back inside and packed a bag for London and Jasmine to spend the weekend with me. After I was done, I grabbed my keys and headed back to the crib. As I drove toward my crib, my mind began to turn. London's birthday was coming up in the next few weeks, and I wanted to get her something special. I had no clue what to get her because she already had every damn thing. Even though London had everything her heart desired, the one thing she didn't have from me was my commitment to her. Was I ready to get married and become a husband to London? I had no clue, but what I did know was that I wanted to do right by her and make her my only girl.

Each day that I looked into her eyes, I felt our connection becoming stronger, and I wanted nothing more than to keep it that way. I was ready to finally step up to the plate to love London like she deserved to be loved. I was ready to put aside the fuckery and the games and give her my all. I was shocked at myself and had no clue where all those feelings had come from. It was like I just woke up one day, and my eyes were opened to what I truly had in front of me. London was being supportive and had gotten out the streets. I had a lovely daughter, who adored me, and I was getting ready to take over Decatur and be the King of the streets.

I was getting everything I asked for, and I was grateful.

Instead of heading home, I made a left and headed to the nearest jewelry store. I didn't hesitate to purchase London a two-thousand-dollar engagement ring to let her know that our love was a promise, and we were soon going to be as one. After leaving the jewelry store, I headed home and put the ring in my drawer until London's birthday came. I knew that once I got down on bended knee, she was going to lose her fucking mind. London had no clue what I was about to give her, and the thrill of her not knowing really had my heart soaring.

# CHAPTER 9

# HARMONY

"Bitch, if you don't answer this damn phone, I swear, when I find your ass again, you going to wish you were never born," Kannon's voice spat into my ear.

I closed my eyes as fear gripped my heart for that brief moment before I deleted the tenth voice message that he had sent me. Kannon had gone from begging me to come back to him to threating my ass. I swear, that nigga was crazy as hell. There was no way I was about to answer any of his calls because I wasn't ready to face his wrath. For three whole days, Kannon continued to blow up my phone and send me messages about how he was going to fuck me up when he saw me again.

Tears fell from my eyes because I knew deep in my heart that if Kannon found me, I was going to be dead even before I could even get a chance to scream for help.

Bria had begged me to come stay with her for a few days, but I quickly told her I was good because I already knew Kannon was going to hit her spot up first looking for me. When Ace told me that I was welcomed to stay as long as I needed, I was grateful as hell. He could have easily put my ass out and told me he didn't want any part of my drama, but he had been by my side every step of the way. I had taken a whole week off work and was just trying to heal my body as well as my mind before I headed back to work.

Bria had come by the house a few times to check on me, and after she saw how Ace was so protective of me, she finally told me that I was probably safer with Ace than at her house anyway.

Ace never took his eyes off me and was constantly ready to fuck a nigga up about me. Even though Ace had come into my life like a knight in shining armor, I still had my doubts and was scared shitless that this fairytale was going to end rather bloody. I was depressed as hell and was barely able to do anything. I hated that I had even gotten myself into this situation. I began to blame myself for being naïve and being hardheaded as hell. I cried myself to sleep every night and woke up with a headache so bad that all I did was lay in bed until the pain would finally subside a few hours later.

It was Saturday, and this was the day that Bria and I normally would go shopping, but from the way I was feeling, I really wasn't in the mood. All I wanted to do was lay in bed and try to figure out what I wanted to do with my life.

I groaned when heard a knock on the door.

"Harmony, are you up? It's five o'clock. I know you should be hungry by now. You have been in the room all day."

"Yes, I'm up."

"Good, I'm taking you out for dinner, so wear something sexy."

"But, I ain't in the mood to go anywhere, and I'm not hungry."

"I don't want to hear it. You been sitting home for three days moping around and barely eating. I'm taking you out. End of discussion."

My heart fluttered as I swung the covers from my half naked body and ran toward the bathroom so I could take care of my hygiene. I stared at myself in the mirror and was shocked to see that I had heavy bags under my eyes, and they still looked bruised. I looked horrible and was scared to come out the room. I didn't hesitate to apply a heavy amount of makeup to cover my dark bruises. I applied some eyeliner, mascara, eyeshadow to my eyes, and some lip-gloss to my full lips. I headed toward the closet and pulled out a pair of white see-through shorts, a black top, and a pair of black flats. I flat ironed my weave so that it was bone straight and sprayed some perfume on my clothes before stepping out the room an hour later.

As I headed toward Ace's room, I noticed his door was closed. I knocked twice, and a few moments later, he opened the door wearing nothing but a towel around his waist. My pussy was aching for some loving, and just seeing this fine ass nigga standing in front of me with hardly any clothes on had me ready to say fuck getting to know a nigga and be a little hoe just one time. I smirked when Ace's eyes began to roam my body. He licked his lips, and my body felt as if it was on fire.

"You looking good, lil' ma."

"Thank you," I whispered.

I swear, I couldn't take my eyes off that nigga the

whole time that he was standing in front of me.

"Give me twenty minutes, and I will be ready," Ace replied with a devious smile on his face.

I began to blush and wanted nothing more than to disappear because I knew I was staring at his ass hard as hell.

"If you want to, you can come in."

I shook my head and took a few steps back until I was practically running down the stairs.

*What the fuck is wrong with me?* I asked myself. Why the fuck was I running from Ace like I was a little girl? Because I knew if I stayed, there was no going out for dinner. He was going to be my dinner, and I wasn't yet ready for shit to go down like that.

It was best to get the fuck out of sight and get my body to calm down before I did some shit that I would later regret. I took a seat on his couch and closed my eyes as I tried to calm myself down, but every time I tried to get my body under control, my pussy got hot again. I was aching for his touch, but I was going to do what I had to do to fight the urge to kiss him and refrain from thinking any nasty thoughts of him. I was willing to do anything to get all the crazy thoughts off my mind.

I shot Bria a message to let her know that Ace was taking me out to eat.

She called my ass up, and I picked up on the first ring.

"Bitch, you showing the fuck out. I'm happy as hell for you. You stay with a fine ass nigga, and he treats your ass like you his girl, and y'all ain't even fucked. But for all I know, you probably fucked his ass the first night you stayed."

I laughed at Bria's crazy ass and denied everything she was saying.

"First off, I didn't fuck him that first night and still haven't fucked him to this day."

"It's okay, sis. If you gave him some pussy, that's your business," Bria joked.

"Bitch, hush. I'm not about to even entertain your ass tonight."

"While you up there trying to think everything through, you need to let your hair down because you single, sis. Get you some dick because I guarantee you if you don't fuck his ass, another bitch will gladly do it for you."

I was just about to tell Bria to mind her own damn business, but that's when Ace decided to come down the stairs.

"Bye, bitch. I got to go."

"Remember what I said, sis. Be a freak, and get nasty as hell. You gonna thank me one day."

I disconnected the call just when Ace and my eyes connected with one another. My heart began to race when I saw just how sexy he was looking.

"Are you ready to go?" he asked me with a sexy grin on his face.

I nodded my head, not really trusting myself to speak. I followed him to the car and slid inside.

The whole ride to the Chipotle Mexican Grill, Ace had his music up, and we listened to Migos as we weaved in and out of traffic. We pulled up at the Mexican grill twenty minutes later and headed inside. We took a seat in a booth in the corner and waited for the waiter to take our order. I found myself staring at Ace throughout most of the date and was contemplating on what Bria had told me over the phone. We enjoyed our food and was just about to leave when a bitch walked up to Ace and smiled in his face. I didn't know the hoe, but when the bitch noticed he wasn't alone, she looked me up and down and turned up her nose at me.

That bitch was about to get her ass fucked up if she even thought for one moment that she was better than me.

"Crystal, what the fuck do you want?" Ace asked the bitch who had just looked at me with disgust.

"I've been trying to call your phone, but I can never reach you."

"Maybe because I blocked your ass. Crystal, what have I told you. Didn't I tell you that we were over with? Why can't you get that through your damn head?" Ace asked with irritation.

I could tell how Crystal was looking that she was mad as hell and was ready to go in on his ass, but Ace quickly dismissed her ass.

"I've been fucking around with your ass for three months, and this how you going to do me? You just going to block me like you and I wasn't fucking just last month?"

Ace's whole demeanor changed.

"Crystal, I enjoyed our time, but it has come to an end. You were just a good time, nothing more. Don't stand here like you fucking care about me because you don't. You just looking for a come up. Don't think I ain't know what you were after. Your free ride is over with. Now, move out my way so I can go."

"Is this supposed to be your new bitch? She ain't even cute," Crystal insulted me.

"Bitch, who the fuck are you talking to? Don't come up in here in your feelings because your used to be nigga is fucking with someone else. If you got a problem, then do something about it. This nigga don't want your ugly ass no more. He's my man now. He will no longer be needing your services. I got everything under control over this way. I'm the new bitch he fucking. I'm the one who sucking and fucking his dick every night while you laying your gold digging ass in bed alone. I'm the one who pushing a brand-new Beamer that he just copped me, and I'm the bitch he one day gonna marry. Now, run along, hoe," I warned.

Even though I was lying through my teeth, the shit

sounded believable because Crystal nutted the fuck up and made the mistake of spitting in my face. I didn't even hesitate to knock fire from the hoe. She had totally disrespected me, and she was about to get her ass beat for that shit. I grabbed the plate that Ace had and slammed it over the bitch's head. Loud screaming broke out, but I wasn't done with the hoe just yet. I was just about to kick the hoe in the face when Ace grabbed me and snatched me away from her.

"You stupid hoe, you can have that little dick ass nigga!" Crystal screamed out.

I was just about to attack her ass again, but Ace had a firm grip on me. Instead, he pulled me out the door, and we hopped in his car. Migos filled the car, but Ace cut it off just before he looked over at me and shook his head.

"Damn, you tore her ass up. I never thought that you were a savage. You didn't show her ass no mercy," Ace joked.

Just listening to him talk about me whooping that bitch's ass had me laughing hard as hell.

"You said a lot of shit back there that I didn't know

about. I didn't know that you had sucked and fucked me."

I laughed so hard my stomach hurt.

"I had to say something to get that bitch mad. She wasn't ever going to get the fuck out your face."

"I have no complaints about anything you did back there, and as far as Crystal goes, she just upset about how shit went down between us. We only fucked around for three months, but the bitch was a big ass gold digger, who was always trying to get to her next dollar. I want something real. I always said when a real one came, I was willing to do whatever I could to make her happy."

My heart began to get warm as his hand began to caress my thigh.

"I'm so glad that we met. You have really come into my life and displayed exactly what a real woman truly is supposed to be."

"How you talking, you acting like you never dated a real woman."

"I have no reasons to lie. I'mma keep it real with you. I've never dated a real one. Even though we ain't known each other long, I can tell that you the real deal… no games and no bullshit."

I totally agreed with everything he was saying. As his hands continued to caress my thighs, my pussy became wetter by the second.

My phone vibrated in my pocket, and I pulled it out only to find out that it was Bria texting me. I laughed when I read her message.

**Bria:** *have you fucked him yet?*

**Me***: No we in the car, but I did have to fuck a bitch up tonight about him.*

**Bria***: Who the fuck you had to fuck up. Bitch call me.*

**Me***: Ima call your nosy ass in the morning and tell you how the shit went down.*

**Bria***: Okay goodnight boo, and have fun.*

**Me***: I will boo.*

When we pulled up at Ace's crib, we hopped out and headed inside. Ace headed straight toward the kitchen and poured us both a small glass of vodka and handed me some lemonade, before he headed upstairs and came back with a small bag of weed. I sipped on my lemonade and vodka while I watched him roll him a fat ass blunt. No words were spoken for the longest as I laid on his shoulder while I sipped on my drink slowly. He grabbed the dominoes from the table, and we started to play a game. I played with him for a while before I felt like I was seeing double. I had refilled my glass so many times that I lost count, and I was feeling that shit in my head. I groaned as I tried to get up and pour me another shot, but my legs buckled, and I fell my ass right back down on the couch.

"Harmony, you might as well sit your ass down because you wasted."

I giggled and placed my leg on his lap and closed my eyes. Weed filled my nose, and I inhaled the scent into my lungs. I groaned as he began to massage my feet. I opened my eyes, and that's when his eyes met mine. I licked my lips and pulled my feet away from him before I scooted closer to him.

I wanted to kiss him, but if I placed my lip on his, I knew that would only lead to us fucking, and I wasn't sure if I was even ready for that shit. We stared deeply into one another's eyes, and I swear I felt our eyes were communicating with one another. He caressed my cheek

190

with his hand before putting out his blunt. He pulled me on top of him, and that's when our lips finally connected. My body felt as if it were on fire as our tongues wrestled with one another. He gently nibbled on my bottom lip as he caressed my neck.

I pulled away first when I felt his hands trying to lift up my shirt. I slid off of him and was about to make a run for it. I was horny as hell, but at the same time, I didn't want him to lose respect for me. I guess he read my mind because he took all the doubt that I was first feeling right away from me. He walked over to where I was standing and told me he didn't want to rush me if I wasn't ready.

"If you want to fuck with me now, then I'm down to break you off this wood, boo. I won't look at you differently. I know you not like these other hoes. You different. But if you ain't ready, I understand. I'm willing to wait on you for however long I have to wait."

I kissed Ace one last time before telling him that I was tired and was going to head to bed. My heart and body were aching for him as I left him and headed to my room. After I had made it to my room, I closed my door and made sure to lock that bitch. I didn't want to even attempt to walk out my room later and make a trip to his room. After I had gotten undressed and had gotten in bed, I tried to sleep, but I couldn't. I heard when Ace came up the stairs and noticed his shadow right outside my bedroom. Just when I thought he was going to knock, he later moved and headed toward his room instead. I sighed with frustration before pulling the covers over my head and falling into a deep sleep.

******

## THE NEXT MORNING

I was knocked the fuck out, but what woke me up was when my phone began to blast Cardi B. I groaned because I already knew who was calling me.

"Bria, it's six in the morning what's wrong, boo?" I asked sleepily.

"Kannon's bitch ass came over here banging on the door asking for you. He looked high as fuck. I told his dumb ass that you weren't in here, but he insisted that he was going to come up in here and try to check me. I had to get Tay up so he could get his ass in check. He better be glad Tay ain't pop his ass, though."

I groaned.

"I'm sorry about that."

"Don't worry, sis. I can handle my damn self. Kannon doesn't scare me. I highly doubt he'll bring his ass back over this way again."

Bri and I talked a little while longer before we both decided to go back to sleep. I was tired as fuck and wasn't in the mood to hear about Kannon's crazy ass. I wanted him to leave me alone, but that wasn't going to happen any time soon. I guess he figured after I hadn't responded to him and hadn't come back home that I was probably hiding out over at Bria's spot. I bet he felt stupid as hell when he found out I wasn't there. I bet he was going crazy wondering where I was at. I closed my eyes and was grateful when sleep found me yet again.

I woke up a few hours later to the smell of pancakes and bacon. My stomach growled as I stepped out of bed and hurried to the bathroom to brush my teeth and comb down my weave. After I had taken care of my hygiene, I made up my bed and slid on my bedroom shoes before I headed downstairs. I had just touched the bottom floor when I noticed Ace standing in the kitchen, flipping over some pancakes, and the smell of coffee filled my nose.

"Morning, sleepy head. How did you sleep?" Ace asked as he glared at me

"Good morning, and I slept good as hell. No hangover either."

Ace chuckled.

"Did you enjoy yourself last night?"

"Yes, I enjoyed dinner until that bitch came in and fucked it up."

"I'm sorry about that."

"It's okay. You can't control other dumb bitches," I mumbled.

I walked over to the coffee pot and poured me a cup of coffee. I needed something to wake my ass up. Ace walked over to where I was pouring my coffee and kissed me on my cheek before taking the coffee pot from my hand and pouring him a cup.

I took a look around, and I swear, I felt like I was home. Staying with Ace had been a wonderful experience so far.

His house was beautiful, and I began to have thoughts about how things would be if I decided to stay. Of course, I knew that wasn't going to happen. I had my own life, and he had his own life as well. There had been no talk about me staying, and I wasn't about to play mind games with myself. This nigga probably only wanted to fuck, and that's it. The plan was to stay with Ace until I could go somewhere else or until Kannon left me the hell alone.

But as I stared over at Ace, I began to wonder if he was going to miss me if I left. I mean, that nigga was cooking me breakfast every morning, fixing me lunch, and even cooking me dinner. Damn, I never thought that I would be in that kind of situation, but people always said that things happened for a reason. If Kannon would never have been beating my ass, I would have never left and met Ace.

I was a grown ass woman, and I felt like I could handle myself and deal with the situation that I found myself in. For almost a week straight, Ace had kept me entertained and had been here every step of the way in the process of being newly single. He catered to my every need and made sure I was comfortable.

Damn, if someone would have told me that I was going to be living with a man who I knew nothing about after breaking up with the man who was supposed to have been my husband, then I wouldn't have believed them. Since I had been staying with Ace, he never did anything to make me feel uncomfortable. After what happened last night, I thought things were going to be awkward this morning, but I didn't feel any bad vibes from him. Even though he kept his hands to himself, I still could see the lust in his eyes.

If Ace wanted the pussy, he was going to have to take things slowly with me. I was still trying to get over the break up with Kannon. I was glad that I had brought my vibrator along with me because I was going to wear that sucker's batteries down, but I remembered what Bria had told me earlier about fucking Ace. If I didn't fuck him, another bitch gladly would.

I saw last night that Ace had that effect on bitches. We were both grown. Whatever happened, would happen, and it was time I stopped trying to prevent shit. I sighed with frustration because here I was playing mind games with myself about whether I should let Ace fuck me or not.

It was time for me to move on from what happened with Kannon and start my new life. We were over with, and there was no reason why I should hold back the chemistry that I was feeling for another nigga. Every time I thought about Kannon, I always seemed to get in a bad mood, and it was too early in the fucking morning to be getting all in my feelings. I was pulled away from my thoughts when Ace fixed me a plate and slid it over to me.

"Thank you for this wonderful meal. I still can't get over the fact that your ass can cook this good," I said before I dug into my food.

"I learned early. I was the only child, and I had to grow up fast so I could help my mom out," Ace replied emotionally.

I chewed slowly as I watched the sadness spread across his face.

"Are you okay?" I asked gently.

"Yes, I'm good. Just thinking about my mom, and how I use to get up every morning and cook for her. Back then, she was so depressed that she could barely even enjoy the meal that I had prepared for her."

I nodded my head and touched his hand.

He quickly pulled away from me, and I could tell that he was hurting.

I didn't want to seem like I was nosy, so I decided to change the subject and talk about something else.

"What are your plans for the day?"

Ace's whole attitude changed, and he came back to his old self.

"I'm heading to the bank to pay the money to purchase that building about three miles from Burger King. I got big plans to open up the next big nightclub. That spot is big enough for the whole damn city to fit in that bitch."

"That sounds good as hell. I'm not the type to do the club scene, but I'm willing to go when it opens to show support."

Ace chuckled.

"Thanks. I would love to have you there. You can go with me if you want."

"I would love that."

I was just about to ask him had he come up with a name for his club when my phone began to vibrate on the table.

I looked down at my phone and noticed it was Kannon calling me. I quickly ignored the shit, and that's when Ace squinted his eyes at me and cleared his throat.

"Is it that nigga calling you?"

I didn't say anything at first because I didn't want to say yes and have Ace flip out like he had when I first came to his crib to stay the night.

My bruises were beginning to heal, but I was still sore. Even though I had taken a whole week off from work, I still walked around the house with my makeup on because I hated for Ace to see me with my bruised face.

"Give me your phone," Ace demanded.

There was no way that I wanted Ace to get my phone, so I tried grabbing it, but Ace was quicker. I watched him as he scrolled throughout my phone, and I noticed his expression had gone from being irritated to angry as hell. My heart began to beat erratically when he stared at me with anger in his eyes.

"This nigga been texting and calling your ass nonstop, and not once did you tell me that this nigga was threatening you."

I was quiet because I had no clue what to say.

"Ace, I didn't tell you because these are my problems. I don't want to get you involved with this shit. Kannon is a damn fool."

"I don't give a fuck about Kannon. I will fuck that nigga up and put him to sleep if he even thinks about laying a hand on you ever again. Why the fuck do you think I told you that it's okay for you to stay here until shit blew over? I've seen bitches getting killed by niggas like Kannon. I don't want your blood on my hands. I brought you here so you wouldn't have to deal with this nigga, but the fact you keeping all this shit secret got my blood boiling."

I closed my eye as Ace fussed at me like I was his fucking child.

"You too damn old to be putting yourself in harm's way. When he was texting your ass and calling you nonstop, all you had to do was let me know, and I would have gone over there and handled his ass."

I stood up and slammed my hands on the table.

"Don't sit here and talk to me like I'm dumb. I'm not your child, and I don't need your protection. I can handle my damn self," I responded with frustration in my voice.

I snatched my phone from his hand and headed out the room. Tears began to fall from my eyes as I stomped up the stairs to my room where I swung open my suitcase and began packing my shit up as fast as I could.

A few moments later, my phone began to ring again. I picked up and didn't even give Kannon time to say shit before I began to blast his ass.

"Nigga, stop calling my fucking phone. Leave me the fuck alone. No, I'm not fucking coming home, and I never want to see your ass ever again. You had six years to get your shit together. Your time is up. I'm done. It's over, nigga. Take that infected dick somewhere else because that shit will never touch this pussy ever again!" I shouted into the phone.

"Bitch, if you don't get your ass home, I will turn this city upside down. Keep fucking with me, Harmony. It ain't over until I say it's over bitch!" Kannon yelled back.

I was about to say more before Ace grabbed my phone and let his presence be known. I stood there in utter shock when he threatened to put a bullet in Kannon's head if he called me ever again.

When he disconnected the call, he handed the phone back to me. He looked at me and then at my bags.

"Where are you going?"

"I'm going to stay with Bria," I mumbled.

"You ain't going nowhere. You safer with me."

I didn't fight him as he began to take all the clothes that I had managed to pack and threw them on my bed.

I was angry and frustrated and just wanted to be left alone. *I am a grown ass woman. I can handle myself. Why in the hell couldn't Ace accept that shit? Because you standing here with bruises all over your body. Admit it to yourself. You can't handle your damn self,* my thoughts argued with me.

"Look, I want to say I'm sorry for going in so hard at you downstairs. I just don't want you to make a mistake by taking this shit lightly. People losing their lives every day from domestic violence. I don't want you to be next because you think this a game. This nigga is crazy. If he says he will fuck you up, Harmony, please believe him. If he comes for you, best believe I will be there to protect you. I can't protect you if you're across town with your friend. Stay here a little while longer until I handle Kannon."

"Handle him? What does that mean?" I asked.

"Nothing your pretty ass need to worry about. Come here for a minute."

I walked slowly over to where he was posted up at, and he embraced me in a hug. When his lips touched my cheek, my knees grew weak, and I felt I was going to fall over. If Ace wouldn't have been holding me, I would have lost my balance and fallen. His touch had me weak, but I tried my best to play it off. He lifted my chin up and told me some shit that I felt in my soul.

"No matter what happens and where this shit leads, I will always be here for you, Harmony. Never forget that shit."

"I won't forget."

He was just about to kiss me when we heard loud banging at his door. My nosy ass followed him downstairs and was shocked to see Jasmine and her father standing at the door. Ace dapped Rocco up before they headed inside.

Jasmine looked up at me, and a smile crossed her face as she wobbled over to where I was standing.

"Hey, pretty little girl," I whispered sweetly in her ear as I embraced her in a tight hug.

Rocco looked from Ace and to me and laughed.

"Nigga, I thought your ass was bullshitting me when you said you had Harmony staying over here."

"I bullshit you not. I told you what the deal was."

Rocco stared over at me and smirked.

"You enjoying yourself with Ace? Have y'all started…"

Ace cut Rocco off real quick, but I wasn't crazy I already knew Rocco was curious and wanted to know if Ace and I were fucking around. I wanted to fuck around with Ace, but at the same time, I was too scared to find out exactly where it was going to lead us.

Rocco and Jasmine chilled out with us for over three hours. We sat around the house and watched cartoons with Jasmine while we all played cards. Of course, Ace beat Rocco and I, but it was a good game. After Rocco had laid Jasmine down for her nap, Rocco and Ace stepped outside on the patio to talk about some shit that I guess they felt like I didn't need to know about.

I sat down on the couch with a bowl of ice cream and watched a Lifetime movie that had me in my feelings. I found myself crying through part of the movie and ended up having to cut the shit off. The suspense was killing me. I wanted to know what Ace and Rocco were talking about that was so important that they had to take their little conversation outside. I tiptoed toward the back of the patio and put my ear to the door so I could hear them.

My whole body went still when I heard Ace talking to Rocco about Kannon. I didn't dare move because I wanted to make sure that I heard every word that was being said. I was so intent on hearing the conversation that I didn't dare breathe. I heard Ace telling Rocco that he was going to murk Kannon if he came near me. When I heard Rocco telling him that he was down, I knew that the shit was real. Ace and Rocco were scheming hard as hell about how they were going to murk Kannon if he contacted me again. My heart grew heavy when Rocco asked Ace how he felt about me. My stomach did a flip as I waited for his answer. When

Ace told Rocco that he was feeling me but he wasn't sure if I felt the same, my emotions were all over the place. He was feeling me, but at the same time, he and I were both sort of holding back. He wasn't coming on too strong because I wasn't giving him the green light that I wanted to take things any further. I took a few steps back from the door, headed back in the living, sat down on the couch, and decided to search within myself to find out if I was ready to give Ace all of me.

******

The few days that I had taken off from work to get my body healed was something I needed. I hated my job with a passion, but I went there and did what I had to do to secure the bag. Now that I didn't have Kannon's money to keep me afloat, I was going to need to keep a job. I woke up, not really in the mood to head to work to deal with Jordan or Mrs. Taylor's petty asses, but I had no other choice. I took my time as I got myself dressed for the day. I looked down at my phone and noticed I was going to be late if I didn't get my ass in the car and leave at that very moment.

I grabbed my purse and knocked on Ace's door to see if he would give me a ride to work.

I knocked on Ace's door once before he opened it and stepped out fully dressed.

"Can you drop me off at work?"

"Of course, that was the plan all along."

I laughed and followed him out the front door. We hopped in his Aston Martin and headed straight to my job. I closed my eyes as I said a silent prayer for what was probably going to be waiting for me when I got there.

"Um, if your ass got to pray every day even before you step foot in that place, then your ass needs to leave that job in the dust."

"I wish I could, but I can't," I mumbled.

"Yes, your ass can. Harmony, what did I tell your ass when you moved into my crib? I told you I got you, and I mean that shit. As soon as I get this club up and running, I promise your ass I'm going to look out for you. I will find something in the club for you to do. Best believe you ain't got to go to work every day to deal with those petty bitches."

My heart soared, and I couldn't help but thank him. I had been struggling my whole fucking life, but all of a sudden, Ace walked in and gave me every ounce of the hope that I lost when I was younger. My childhood was horrible, and my adult life wasn't any damn better. I blamed my damn mama for abusing me. If her ass would have given me the proper love and nurturing that I needed growing up, there was no way would I have ever fallen for Kannon.

I would have run from his ass, but Kannon was all I knew. My mama wasn't any better. After she was killed a few years back, I felt some type of relief, but I never got any closure on why she was so abusive. Was it because my dad left her when she was pregnant with me, ran off, and married some other hoe? Was it because I looked like him, and I reminded her of her mistake? I didn't know what it was, but all I knew was she didn't make life easy for me, and since I'd been grown, I was still trying to get my life on track and detach myself from toxic relationships.

When we pulled up at my job, Ace grabbed me and placed a kiss on my lips.

"Have a good day. I will drop by and pick you up so we can have lunch together."

"That sounds amazing."

As soon as I headed into the building, Jordan's nosy ass was waiting for me. I hoped she wasn't about to start no shit because I was ready to curse her ass out.

"Harmony, I'm glad that you're back."

I looked at the fake bitch but didn't bother responding. I wasn't in the mood to deal with her.

"Your boyfriend came two days straight looking for you. That nigga fine as hell. If you don't want him anymore, I would love to take him off your hands."

I clenched my teeth and turned around to face her ass.

"Sweetheart, I don't give a fuck what you do. Now, do me a favor, and leave me the fuck alone." I growled.

Jordan didn't speak. I swear, if she would have uttered one word, I would have hit that bitch in her throat. I barely got through work that day. God was definitely on my side, and I was going to give him all the praise. From Mrs. Taylor talking shit to me and Jordan being fake, I was close to pulling my hair out and was thinking hard about not even coming back after I took my lunch break. When I took the job, I really thought that the kids were going to be rough, but the kids hadn't given me any problems, and neither did any of the parents. The only problem I had was with my supervisor and Jordan's lying ass. They were driving me up the wall with their pettiness. When the clock struck twelve, I grabbed my bag and was ready to dip the fuck out, but I wasn't expecting to walk outside to find Kannon posted up waiting for me.

I was frozen with fear because I didn't think that Kannon and I were going to be standing face to face ever again, especially not so soon. He must have seen the fear that was on my face because he laughed. His laugh was evil and made me want to scream out in fear. He walked over to me and tried to touch me, but I snatched away from his ass which only pissed him off.

"If you thought for even a moment that I was going to let you go, then you are sadly mistaken. It ain't over, bitch. Now, be a good girl, and get in the fucking car."

Even though I was scared, I wasn't about to let that nigga punk me out like I was some type of weak bitch. That

210

nigga had come to my job, thinking he was about to scoop me up, and it wasn't going to happen. If he even thought about grabbing my ass, I was ready to light a fire to his ass and scream my head off. The daycare that I worked at was right down the road from the police station I already knew he didn't want that heat to come to his doorstep. I took a few steps back from his ass.

"I ain't going no damn where with your ass. You and I are over with. Why can't you accept the shit?"

The whole time that Kannon and I were fussing, I was praying that Ace would hurry the hell up and come fuck Kannon up one good time. I wanted that nigga out of my life, and there was no way he was going to do that as long as he breathed. As soon as he snatched my arm, I spotted Ace's Aston Martin pull up next to Kannon's Rolls Royce. Ace stepped out the car, and it was a wrap.

"Nigga, what I tell your ass? I told you that I better not catch your ass around Harmony, and here your thirsty ass is!" Ace yelled.

"Who the fuck are you? Oh, never mind. I see you that greasy ass motherfucka who was talking all that shit over the phone. Let me tell you something, nigga, Harmony is my damn bitch. She belongs to me."

"Hold the fuck up, nigga. I don't belong to your ass. Ace is my man now. You had six years to get your shit together, but what did you do? You fucked all these hoes and beat my ass on the regular. Let's not forget about them herpes that you caught and lied about having. Nigga, I will never be with your ass again." I huffed.

I must have hit a nerve because Kannon tried to grab my ass, and that's when Ace laid Kannon's ass out. He didn't say shit but aimed straight for his nose. Kannon cried out in pain. Kannon's passenger door opened, and I spotted Young G. I should have known that Kannon didn't bring his thirsty ass to my job by himself.

"Get your hands off my nigga, homie!" Young G yelled out.

When Ace and Young G's eyes connected, shit really got real.

"Oh, hell nall. I should have known your slimy ass had something to do with this," Ace sneered.

"I don't know what the fuck you talking about. Kannon

my nigga. He and I been rocking for a minute. How was I to know y'all were beefing?" Young G argued.

I could tell how Ace was looking at Young G that they had bad blood with one another. Young G squinted his eyes at Ace and walked toward him like he was ready to throw them hands.

"Nigga, I can tell you in your fucking feelings about that Rocco shit. Don't hate, nigga, because we getting money. You can join my team. We winning. Don't be hating because you don't have the type of connections like I do. I can take Rocco places that your ass can't take him. I'm doing something that you can't do, and that's getting his ass paid."

"I don't give a fuck about what you and Rocco got going on. I don't want any part of the shit. But I know one thing... nothing better not happen to my lil' bro. Because if it does, I swear to you that I will slit your throat!" Ace roared.

Kannon held on to his bloody nose and watched as Young G and Ace continued to chew each other out. Next thing I know, I heard my supervisor screaming that she was about to call the police. Kannon and Young G hopped in the car and dipped the fuck out of there.

Mrs. Taylor squinted her eyes at me before telling me that I was fired.

"Whatever you got going on with your personal life need to stay away from your job. For a week straight, your little boyfriend kept coming by asking about you. Now that you back, he comes back and causes a scene. You can't work here, bringing all this drama to my center."

I looked at her like she was crazy as hell. The fact that the bitch fired me on my lunch break and didn't even give me time to explain what had just gone down confirmed that she wanted to get rid of me for a long time. She just didn't have any reason to fire me back then.

I stood there with an open mouth as I watched her bad body ass walk back into the building. Ace held me as tears began to fall from my eyes.

"Baby, don't cry. I got you. I promise you that. You hated this job anyway. Consider it a blessing that she fired you. Come on. Let's get the fuck out of here. I'm taking your sexy ass shopping, and if you want, I can give you some of this dope dick to put your mind at rest."

I pulled away from him and laughed until my stomach hurt. I wiped the tears from my eyes as I followed him to the car. How I was feeling, I was down to go shopping and finally bless Ace with some of my pussy.

# CHAPTER 10

## ACE

The fact that Kannon and Young G knew one another didn't sit well with me. The only thing I could think about was fucking those niggas up before they came for me. I saw how Kannon looked at me. His ass wasn't about to give up that easily. He was going to want to fight dirty, and the fact that Young G and I had bad blood put me in a complicated position. It even had me more concerned about Rocco. As soon as I got home, I was going to hit Rocco's line up to let him know what was up. I looked over at Harmony, and it seemed like she was in a deep thought. I caressed her thigh, and she finally smiled at me.

"Thanks for what you did back there."

"I got you, boo. There was no way I was about to let that lame ass nigga put his hands on ya or take you anywhere. I was ready to murk a nigga back there."

"Yeah, I can tell you were. I was scared for you."

"No reason to be scared, boo. I can handle myself."

"That nigga back there... Young G. How you know him?"

"He went to high school with me and Rocco. We all was cool until he snitched on one of my homies, and he got locked up. He serving a twenty-year bid."

"I never liked his ass, every time he hung around Kannon, I noticed Kannon's attitude was always more aggressive and reckless toward me."

"Young G ain't shit but a snitch. I never got a good feeling about his snake ass, but Rocco swear up and down that Young G can be trusted."

Harmony snorted.

"I highly doubt Young G is trustworthy. He looks slimy if he ain't."

"Back in the day, Young G was sort of fat, tall, and was dark skinned. He wasn't the most attractive nigga, but he pulled a lot of bitches back then because they were after his paper."

Now that we were all in our early thirties and fully grown, Young G had slimmed down and was rocking some dreads.

"Like I said earlier, Young G wouldn't be shit if he didn't have money, and the bitches wouldn't even be bothered by his ass."

A few moments later, I pulled up at my crib, and Harmony and I hopped out. I followed Harmony in the house and watched as she headed straight to the kitchen and started cooking dinner. I took that time to pull out my phone so I could hit Rocco up. I was grateful when he picked up on the first ring.

"Bro, guess who I ran into today?"

"Who?"

"That slimy ass nigga Young G. Turns out, Young G is Kannon's right-hand nigga. Kannon and him pulled up on Harmony at her job today and tried to snatch her ass up. I was about to lay buddy ass out today."

"Bro, so you telling me that Young G and Harmony's ex cool?"

"Yeah, nigga, they cool."

Rocco became quiet, and I didn't know if that was a good thing or a bad thing.

"Ace, I know you don't like Young G, but I can't just stop fucking with Young G. Tonight, we make our first drop, and I'm expecting to get some serious bread. It's too

218

late in the game to turn back now."

I sighed with frustration. There was no way I was about to stay on the phone with Rocco any longer than I had to. I quickly disconnected the call and headed upstairs. I had never been the type to leave the house not strapped, but it had been the first time that I didn't have my Glock on me. I was going to make sure I kept a piece on me at all times because niggas like Kannon weren't going to chill. They were going to keep on doing fuck shit to get under my skin until I snapped and started blazing my guns at their asses. Whenever the nigga came for me, I was going to be ready. If Young G wanted to get involved, I had enough bullets to put his ass to sleep also.

******

### 2 WEEKS LATER

Signing my name on the dotted line and owning my own club had finally come true. No longer was it a damn dream; it was a reality. For two weeks straight, I had busted my ass and barely slept because I was doing what I could to make sure that my club was on point. I had interviewed over fifty employees that I was going to hire and bring

219

them all in for training. Starting your own business was a challenge, but I was down to get the challenge accomplished. Harmony had been there every step of the way and had been going out of her way by interviewing the women that I was interested in hiring. Since she was no longer working her job at the daycare, she spent her days with me, trying to get my club together.

Harmony had already started doing ads around Decatur, and people were getting hyped as hell that I was about to bring a nightclub to the area. I mean, it wasn't about to be one of those small, ghetto ass clubs. My club was going to be where Gucci Mane would want to come and chill. It was going to be just that damn dope.

A soft knock on the door pulled me away from my daze. Harmony stepped into my office wearing a pair of tight skinny jeans, a pair of all black Jordans, and a white top. She had her weave pulled back in a bun, and she was holding some folders in her hand.

"Baby, I just wanted to bring you these folders on the employees that I just interviewed. I liked all fifty of them, and half of them already have club experience."

I lit me a blunt and motioned for her to come closer to me. I blew the smoke out my nose before she took a seat on my lap. Our lips met one another, and my dick instantly got on hard.

"Damn, nigga, I see your ass done got excited."

"Man, I always get excited by your sexy ass," I whispered in her ear. "Thank you, baby, for being here with me."

"I wouldn't want to be anywhere else."

I stared into her eyes, and I knew instantly she was telling me the truth. The fact I had a strong independent woman working beside me had me feeling good as hell. I was no longer tackling the world alone. I had a companion who was just as passionate about being a business owner as I was. We were perfect for one another. I felt in my heart that I had finally found the woman I was supposed to spend the rest of my life with. Harmony and I had been so busy working and grinding to get our paper up that we had been neglecting going out and spending time with one another. I couldn't even remember the last time that we had gone out with one another. The fact that we still haven't had sex only told me one thing—we had a bond that was unbreakable.

If she would have been any other bitch, I would have smashed her on the first night, but Harmony was better than that, and I treated her like the queen that she was.

I wanted to do something special for Harmony. For the first time, I wanted the night to be all about us. I groaned when I looked down at my computer, and I began calculating the monthly cost of keeping the club running.

"There is so much to do and not enough hours in a day," I mumbled to myself.

"Don't stress about it baby. We going to get it done. Harmony whispered into my ear before placing a kiss on my cheek.

She stood up and looked at her watch before asking me what I wanted for lunch. I had been working so hard that I had almost forgotten to damn eat. I glanced over at the clock and noticed it was three in the afternoon. I stretched my arms for a brief moment before I pulled out my wallet and handed her thirty dollars. I got a taste for some Chinese.

Harmony's eyes lit up. Chinese was her favorite food so we were always eating Chinese or either Mexican food.

"Okay I will go pick up something to eat and I will be right back."

I nodded my head at her before I got back to work.

When my phone started to ring, I grabbed it out of my pocket and was shocked to see Rocco's name on my screen. Rocco and I had both been grinding so much that we had gone close to two weeks without speaking or checking up on each other. He was doing his own thing, and I was doing mine.

"Bro, where you at? Damn, I ain't heard shit from you in almost two weeks," Rocco stated.

"I know. I have been grinding, trying to get the club opened up. Harmony and I been working hard as hell."

"Damn, you and Harmony sure is close. I see you got you a ride or die."

"Yes, she different than all them other hoes. Harmony is real as they come. She's my damn queen."

"I never thought I would hear you say some shit like that, but I'm happy for you, bro. You are living your dream, and you got you a real one."

"Thank you, bro. How things been going with you and London?"

"Everything been going good. You know her birthday is next month. Bro, I'ma ask her to marry me."

I was speechless as hell. I mean, I couldn't even fix my mouth to say shit for the longest moment.

"Ace, you there, nigga?"

"Yes, I'm here," I managed to choke out.

"Did you hear me?"

"Yes, I heard your ass. Damn, nigga, I can't believe that shit. Are you being serious?"

"Hell yeah, bro. I already bought her the ring. It was about two thousand dollars. We ain't getting any younger, and she the mother of my child. She crazy about my ass, and I'm crazy about her ass too. I don't see myself with anybody else. We been through a lot of shit this year, but if I had to choose a bitch to make mine, I would have to choose her every time. These past few months, we have done some fucked up shit to one another, but after Dad died, none of those hoes was there for me, except London.

She went over and beyond and held me down, and for that, I have nothing but loyalty to her. I was so depressed that I didn't even want to get out of bed, but London came to check on my ass every day. It's funny how she used to stress me but then turned around and helped heal me."

"Rocco, I never thought that you would be getting married before me, but I'm more than happy for you. The fact London held you down like she did shows you that her love for you was real from the jump. If no one else deserves the ring, then she does. I'm glad you leaving the hoes alone and settling down. I wish you nothing but happiness."

"Thanks, bro. Dad would be so proud of us if he was still here."

My heart began to break when he mentioned my uncle. Damn, I hated that he wasn't there to see just what I was about to do with myself. The only thing that kept me sane was knowing he was up in heaven watching down on me.

**\*\*\*\***

Harmony and I didn't leave the club until after ten that night. Harmony yawned as I swerved in and out of traffic as I hurried home. I could tell she was tired, but I wanted us to do something special tonight. As soon as I pulled up at my house, we both hopped out the car and headed inside. I hurried toward her bathroom and ran her some bathwater and poured her favorite scented bubble bath liquid in the tub. I called Harmony in the bathroom, and she came in a few moments later with a bottle of wine and a wine glass.

"Thank you, baby. You read my damn mind. You just don't know how much my body been feening for a bubble bath."

I chuckled and took a seat on the toilet as I watched her undress. I couldn't help but stare at her sexy body as she slid into the tub. I poured her a glass of wine and watched as she placed her lips on the glass and drank the contents of the glass. I didn't hesitate to start massaging her shoulders and neck as she sipped her wine and relaxed in her bubble bath. When I flicked my tongue over her earlobe, she moaned out my name before turning around and slipping her tongue into my mouth. Her wet hands caressed my chest and pushed my head farther down toward her as we deepened the kiss. A few moments later, she stood her dripping wet body from the tub and wrapped herself in a big black towel before we headed into our bedroom.

My dick was rising, and I was harder than a brick. I wasn't expecting her to remove the towel and push me down on the bed. I licked my lips as I waited to see what she was about to do next. I wanted to touch her, but she pushed my hands away. Instead, she pulled down my pants and boxers, and I pulled off my shirt. I groaned when her hands began to stroke my dick up and down just before she slid it into her mouth.

"Fuck," I moaned as she began to slurp and suck on my dick like it was the best that she had ever tasted.

She was sucking me so damn good that I didn't even have to guide her on what to do. As she sucked and licked on the head of my dick, I played with her titties. She gave me mind-blowing head that had a nigga's toes curling. I wanted nothing more than to please her sexy ass, but Harmony had her own plans. Just when I thought she was done with pleasing me, she slid on top of my rock-hard dick and began to slowly grind on me. I clenched my teeth as her tight pussy gripped my dick. I squeezed her little ass as she began to speed up and began to fuck me harder.

I reached for her titties as she bounced up and down on my pole. Her cries were music to my ears and only had me wanting to slam into her a few times. She pushed my arms toward the top of my head as she began to clench her pussy muscles on my dick. She was fucking a nigga so good that she had me moaning her name. I had never moaned a bitch's name, but as she popped her pussy on a nigga, I had no other choice. Every time she clenched her pussy muscle, I wanted to cum, but I was doing my best to hold back.

"Cum for me, daddy," she moaned in my ear as she leaned down on my chest.

When I heard her scream into my ear and her body began to shake, I grabbed her by her hips and slammed into her a few times before I flipped her ass over, pushed her face in the pillow, and entered her from the back. She clenched the sheets with her hand as I began to pound her little pussy. She screamed out my name like it was chant as I drilled her.

I yanked her hair in a tight grip as I slammed into her a few more times just before I caught my nut.

After we were done, we laid down next to one another, and no words were spoken. To be honest, Harmony had fucked me so damn good that she had me speechless. When her hands began to caress my chest, I turned over and looked her in the eyes.

"That was amazing," I told her truthfully.

She smirked.

"Skinny girls still winning, baby."

I laughed at her crazy ass and smacked her on her little booty.

"Baby, I don't know where this going, but I pray you and I are on the same page. I never thought I could love another man after Kannon, but when I met you, you opened my eyes to what a real man is. These feelings that I have for you aren't letting up and are getting stronger every day. The love and respect that I have in my heart for you have me wanting to give you my all. I feel safe with you, and there is no other place that I'd rather be."

To hear her say all that shit had me in my feelings

because I damn sure was feeling the same way. I wasn't about to push her, but I wanted to give her the time and space to figure out exactly what she wanted to do. There was no way I wanted to pressure her into loving me or even waiting to be with me. I wanted her to feel it within her soul, and now that we were on the same page, I was willing to give her all of me if she was willing to give me all of her.

"Baby, you and I are on the same page. You have nothing to worry about. Your heart is safe with me. If you promise to give me all of you, I will give you all of me in return."

"I promise," she murmured.

I didn't let her say anything more. I wanted to show Harmony just how much she meant to me, and I was willing to do whatever I could to let her know that no matter what, she was all I needed and wanted.

*****

## A MONTH LATER

Tonight was a huge success, and Black City was deep

as fuck. The fact that it was my opening night, and I had persuaded Migos to make a club appearance was what brought everyone from Decatur and surrounding areas to my spot. VIP was popping upstairs while downstairs was crowded with everyone dancing, smoking, and just having a good time. I stood back and was amazed at what me and Harmony had accomplished.

"Thank you, baby, for helping me out with making my dream come true."

Harmony placed her small hand on my face before pulling me down and placing a kiss on my lips.

"You just don't know how happy you have made me. I'm glad to call you my man."

Hearing her say that shit set my soul on fire.

I was just about to whisper some sexy shit in her ear when I heard my name being called. I looked around, and there stood Rocco. The grill in his mouth gleamed as he smiled at me and dapped me up. He pulled Harmony into a hug before turning back to me.

"I didn't think you were going to come through."

"Nigga, you should know there was no way I was about

to miss your club opening."

Rocco looked around and started talking about how much he liked the setup. When the DJ yelled out that Migos was in the building, the club went crazy. Next thing you knew, everyone heard Migos' "Get Right Witcha."

"This my damn song!" Harmony screamed before she began to slowly grind on my dick.

I was enjoying Harmony twerking so much that I wasn't paying any attention when Kannon walked his thirsty ass over to where we were posted up at. When I heard Harmony scream, it was too late.

*Pow. Pow. Pow.*

I pushed Harmony out the way and started firing back.

Screaming filled the club as everyone tried to get the fuck out of there. I tried running after Kannon, but it wasn't any use. The nigga came up in there, shot up my damn club, and had dipped right back out.

I was furious and was ready to fuck that nigga up, but first, I had to find Rocco. I ran back to where he was. I could hear the ambulance and police in the distance as I pushed through the crowd. My heart fell out my chest when I found Harmony on her knees covered in Rocco's blood. Tears were falling from her eyes as she looked up at me.

"He's dead, Ace."

"No, it can't be. We were just talking."

"Get up, Rocco, and stop playing," I sobbed.

I shook his body, but Rocco didn't move. Harmony held me as I cried for the nigga who was like a brother to me.

"This was all my damn fault. I was supposed to have protected him!" I kept screaming out loud.

"Please forgive me, Uncle Dro," I cried.

I was so caught up in my feelings that I didn't even hear the paramedics come in. They pushed me aside as they tried to perform CPR, but it was too late. My cousin was gone. I wiped the last of my tears from my eyes before Harmony and I left the club. The whole ride home, I said nothing. There was nothing to say, and I was grateful that Harmony didn't say shit either. I was pissed the fuck off and was ready to murk a nigga.

When we pulled up at the crib, I didn't get out the car

right then. Instead, I turned to her and looked her dead in the eye.

"My damn cousin is fucking gone, and Kannon is the bitch ass nigga who pulled the trigger."

No tears left my eyes. I was all cried out.

"Baby, I'm so sorrr…"

I cut her off.

"I want to know where I can find Kannon. I'm going to put a bullet in that nigga's head from taking the only family that I have."

Harmony didn't speak fast enough, which pissed me off.

I clenched my teeth, balled up my fist, and punched the dashboard.

"Harmony, don't sit here and play with me. Give me the information that I need."

Harmony began to cry, but I didn't have time to try to wipe her tears. I had only one thing in mind, and that was to put Kannon six feet deep.

When she finally gave me Kannon's address, I typed it in my phone and told Harmony to head inside, and that I would be back later. Harmony began to cry harder.

"Please, baby, don't go do nothing crazy."

"Baby, I will be back. Just go in the house. I have to go talk to London and let her know what happened."

Harmony slid out the car a few moments later, and I waited until she made it in the house before I pulled out the driveway. The whole ride to Rocco's baby mama's house, I had no clue on how I was going to tell her that her baby daddy was dead. I felt weak as hell, but after I pulled up at London's spot, I slid out my car and knocked on her door.

It was three in the morning, but London managed to open the door for me. I stared down at her, and my heart broke yet again.

"Ace, what you doing here so late? Where's Rocco?"

"London, I came over here to let you know that Rocco is gone," I choked out.

"What?" London asked emotionally.

"He came by the club, and a nigga came in and was shooting. He got hit in the chest. He died instantly."

London screamed and yelled as she hit me over and over until she fell down on the floor.

"Rocco!" she kept screaming.

I got down on my knees and held her tightly while she cried until she couldn't cry any longer. She sniffled and wiped her tears as she pulled away from me.

"Who killed him? Where were you at?'

"I know who killed him, and I promise you that Rocco is going to get justice."

London didn't say anything for the longest time.

"Jasmine is going to be so hurt. She too young to understand her daddy is never coming back," London mumbled.

London took a few steps back from me before she closed the door in my face.

I sighed and headed back to my crib. London and I both took Rocco's death hard. I had no clue if London was ever going to get over it either.

"I promise you, Rocco, that I'm going to get justice for you. I will make sure London and Jasmine are well taken care of. Rest, Rocco, because I'm going to handle this shit down here."

## A FEW DAYS LATER

It was the day of Rocco's funeral, and I had no clue if I was going to be able to make it. It was way too emotional. If it wasn't for Harmony, I don't know how I would have gotten through the last few days. I had spent the past few days cleaning up Rocco's house, packing his shit up, and giving most of it away because I couldn't stand looking at any of it. When I ran across the engagement ring that he had purchased for London's birthday, my heart broke in half. My plan had been to give it to London when I saw her again. I was sure that Rocco would have wanted her to have it. The ring that was in my pocket felt heavy and weighed my pocket down.

I stared at myself in the mirror, but I still couldn't get my emotions together to go to the funeral. A loud knock interrupted me.

"Baby, are you ready?"

I sighed but told Harmony that I was dressed and ready.

Harmony drove us to the church, and I remained silent. I didn't say one word. When we pulled up at the church thirty minutes later, we stepped out the car and headed inside. Rocco was well known in the streets, and the church was deep as hell. I took a seat on the front row by London and Jasmine. The funeral was sad as hell, and everyone was crying and screaming. London held on to me as she cried out Rocco's name. Harmony looked over at me and held my hand tightly.

After the funeral was over, we headed to the gravesite and put Rocco in the ground. As the pastor said a small prayer and ended the ceremony, I grabbed London by her arm and told her that Rocco had left her something.

I pulled out the small box from my pocket, and London grabbed it from me with shaky hands. When she opened it, she began to cry.

"He told me just before he died that he was going to ask you to marry him on your birthday."

London cried loudly, and I held her as she wet my shirt up. Harmony stood back in the distance and watched us. She pulled the ring out the box and slid it on her finger.

"No matter what happens, you will always have my heart, Rocco," London whimpered.

London looked up at me.

"Have you murked that nigga who took Rocco's life?"

"No, I haven't, but I know where he at. I'm going to take care of it. Don't worry about it. Rocco going to get his justice."

London nodded her head at me and told me that I was welcome to come see Jasmine anytime I wanted to.

"Thanks, London. I'm always going to be in Jasmine's life."

I kissed Jasmine on her cheek and waved bye to her.

Harmony walked over to me and wrapped her hands in mines.

*****

I slid out of bed when I heard the sound of Harmony snoring. I quickly got dressed and headed out the house. I pulled up the address that Harmony had given me the night that Rocco was killed. It was a thirty-minute drive, but it was going to be so worth it. I rode in silence the whole time. When I got close to Kannon's spot, I sat in my car down the road. I tried getting myself together. I wanted

Kannon dead, and I was willing to do anything to see that nigga bleed.

I grabbed my gun from my glove compartment, loaded that bitch up, and jogged up the road to that nigga's house. I noticed he had company, but I didn't give a fuck. I was willing to shoot up his whole family if I needed to. As soon as I ran up in his yard, I headed straight to his door and kicked that bitch in. I heard nothing but bitches screaming, and I started blasting my gun. The smell of weed filled my nose as the naked bitches ran out the back door. Nobody was left but Kannon and Young G, who was laying on the floor coughing up blood.

I walked over to Kannon and looked down at his ass. Blood spluttered from his mouth as I took one last look at him.

"Nigga, you think I was about let you live after you took my lil' bro away from me? I will see your ass in hell," I muttered vehemently before pulling the trigger three times.

I walked over to Young G and didn't hesitate to shoot his ass in the fucking head also. I dipped out the house as fast as I had come and headed back home. When I stepped back in my house, I quickly undressed and took a hot shower before getting back in bed under Harmony.

"Baby," Harmony whined

"What's wrong, boo?"

"I love you."

When Harmony confessed her love to me, my whole world had a fucking purpose. Yes, I had lost my uncle, who was like a father to me, and I had just lost my cousin, who was just like a lil' bro to me, but I wasn't alone, even though my heart was broken.

When Harmony's lips connected with my own, I knew in my heart that as long as she and I stuck it out together, we would go far in life, and I would never ever be alone ever again.

# A YEAR LATER...

"Bitch you about to shut this whole wedding down," Bria joked as she took a few pictures of me.

I was rocking a long crème wedding gown that fitted my curves as well as hugged my baby bump. I was now five months pregnant, but a bitch was glowing. Never would I have ever thought that I would be marrying the man of my dreams and having his baby. Life was so crazy. Last year I had no clue where I was going or even if I was going to survive to even live to see another day. I thanked God every day for opening up my eyes and showing me exactly what I was dealing with and protecting me when I didn't know I needed protection.

My love for Ace was stronger than ever. He was everything that I ever wanted in a man and there was no other nigga that I wanted to be with. I was planning on spending the rest of my life with Ace and our child.

Ace and I was living the good life. After Rocco was killed Ace wanted to give up on the night club, but there was no way I was about to allow the man I loved to go back to the street life. Instead I held my man down and helped him out of his depression only for him to come back on top. We were winning again and there was no stopping us. "Black City" was making so much money that all type of famous rappers and singers was up in that bitch on the daily. Black City was talked about so much that even the shade room had did an interview with Ace to ask how his club had gotten so damn successful. I was proud of my baby because through all the pain and heart ache him and I had overcome all the bullshit.

As I stared at myself in the mirror I noticed Bria standing behind me with a smile on her face.

"I'm so happy for you, you deserve this shit and more," she mumbled before I turned around and was embraced in a tight hug by her.

I rubbed on my baby bump one last time, before I grabbed the side of my dress and followed Bria out the door.

My palms were sweating, and I was nervous as hell, but I closed my eyes and counted to ten to calm myself down. A few moments later I heard the music starting to play and that's when the church doors opened up. The church was deep as hell, but I wasn't bothered by anyone but the man whom I was about to spend the rest of my life with. I didn't dare take my eyes off of him as I walked down the long aisle. When I finally made it to the altar, he pulled my veil from my face and stared into my eyes.

"You're so beautiful," he muttered.

"Thank you," I blushed.

My heart began to flutter when it was time for him to put my ring on my finger. The ring was gorgeous, and I fell in love with it instantly. After we had exchanged rings, I waited for the ultimate kiss to seal the deal.

Loud clapping and cheering followed as he caressed my cheek and placed his lips on mine. Everyone disappeared and nothing else mattered but him and I. He pulled away from me for only a brief moment.

"I love you and the baby so much. I promise to love y'all both until the day I die."

If I didn't know nothing else I knew what Ace said to me was the truth. My heart and mind were at peace because I knew in my soul that Ace wouldn't never break my heart.

# The End

# CONNECT WITH ME ON SOCIAL MEDIA

- **Send me a friend request on Facebook:**
https://www.facebook.com/profile.php?id=100011411930304&__nodl

- **Like my author's page on Facebook:**
https://www.facebook.com/ShaniceBTheAuthor/?ref=settings

- **Join my reader's group. I post short stories and sneak peeks of my upcoming novels that I'm working on:**
**https://www.facebook.com/groups/1551748061561216/**

- **Visit www.shaniceb.com to subscribe to my website and my mailing list.**

- **Follow me on Instagram:**

**shaniceb24**

# ABOUT THE AUTHOR

Shanice B was born and raised in Georgia. At the age of nine years old, she discovered her love for reading and writing. At the age of ten, she wrote her first short story and read it in front of her classmates, who fell in love with her wild imagination. After graduating high school, Shanice decided to pursue her career in early childhood education. After giving birth to her son, Shanice decided it was time to pick up her pen and get back to what she loved the most.

She is the author of eighteen books and is widely known for her bestselling four-part series titled *Who's Between The Sheets: Married To A Cheater.* Shanice is also the author of a three-part series titled *Love Me if You*

*Can*, three standalones titled *Stacking It Deep: Married To My Paper*, *A Love So Deep: Nobody Else Above You*, and *Love, I Thought You Had My Back*. In November of 2016, Shanice decided to try her hand at writing a two-part street lit series titled *Loving my Mr. Wrong: A Street Love Affair*. Shanice resides in Georgia with her family and her five-year-old son.

Be sure to <u>LIKE</u> our Major Key

Publishing page on Facebook!

CPSIA information can be obtained
at www.ICGtesting.com
Printed in the USA
LVHW011657180119
604419LV00014B/579/P